“Why didn’t you tell me I had a daughter?”

His gaze burned into hers, as if he could see inside her tattered heart.

“Frankly, I didn’t plan to ever tell you. But then I saw you on the news and I thought…”

“You thought I might die and Chrissy would never know her father.” He ran a hand through his hair. “A daughter… I can’t believe it.”

Katie tried to forget all the hurt and resentment she felt toward Reese. But it pained her to know that he’d never wanted her. Then or now.

“Back then I was young and thoughtless,” he said. “Now all I can do is ask for your forgiveness.”

She didn’t trust Reese. But she knew she had to try. “It’s in the past.”

“Not for me. I just found out that I’m a father. I need time to adjust.”

She didn’t want him adjusting. Frankly, she didn’t know what she wanted. All she knew was that she didn’t want trouble. But as she looked at Reese, she was certain trouble was unavoidable.

Leigh Bale is a *Publishers Weekly* bestselling author. She is the winner of the prestigious Golden Heart® Award and is a finalist for the Gayle Wilson Award of Excellence and the Booksellers' Best Award. The daughter of a retired US forest ranger, she holds a BA in history. Married in 1981 to the love of her life, Leigh and her professor husband have two children and two grandkids. You can reach her at leighbale.com.

Books by Leigh Bale

Love Inspired

Men of Wildfire

Her Firefighter Hero
Wildfire Sweethearts
Reunited by a Secret Child

Lone Star Cowboy League

A Doctor for the Nanny

The Road to Forgiveness
The Forest Ranger's Promise
The Forest Ranger's Husband
The Forest Ranger's Child
Falling for the Forest Ranger
Healing the Forest Ranger
The Forest Ranger's Return
The Forest Ranger's Christmas
The Forest Ranger's Rescue

Visit the Author Profile page at Harlequin.com for more titles.

Reunited by a Secret Child

Leigh Bale

HARLEQUIN® LOVE INSPIRED®

Recycling programs for this product may not exist in your area.

ISBN-13: 978-1-335-50945-1

Reunited by a Secret Child

This edition published by arrangement with Love Inspired Books.

www.Harlequin.com

Printed in U.S.A.

Wait on the Lord: be of good courage,
and he shall strengthen thine heart:
wait, I say, on the Lord.
—*Psalms* 27:14

To Nancy, Joyce, Sally and Debbie…
my childhood friends. We sure had some
fun times, didn't we?

Chapter One

Wide, yellow ribbons fluttered among the cottonwoods bordering the north perimeter of the tarmac. The low hum of the prop plane's engine escalated Reese Hartnett's tension. Gazing out the small, oval window inside the plane, he gripped the armrests with tensed fingers. He'd been raised here, in the sleepy little town of Minoa, Nevada, but it wasn't his home anymore. He had no family here now. No friends, either. But he didn't know where else to go.

And honestly, he'd felt compelled to return. After what he'd been through, he longed to see his mom. If only she were still alive. Coming home was the best way to be close to her again. To go to the cemetery to pay his respects and apologize for hurting her when he'd left so unexpectedly.

He squinted as a spray of morning sunlight glinted against the metal siding of the hangar. Someone had tied a large hand-painted sign across the front of the building. He could easily make out the words: *Welcome home. Our hero.*

Reese knew the sign was for him. No doubt the media had put it up, staging a warm greeting in hopes of getting his story. He sure didn't believe the people of this town had put up the sign. Not when they remembered his past history as a juvenile delinquent. Nor did he feel like a hero. Not when his entire hotshot crew had died two weeks earlier, fighting a wildfire in Colorado. Nineteen members of the Garlock Hotshot Crew should still be here with him. His buddies. Laughing and joking. Inseparable.

Because Reese had been the lone survivor, everyone considered him brave. But he wasn't. He was just an ordinary man who happened to survive. Even now, he could see no logical reason why he had lived when all his friends had died. And every night, he hoped he'd awaken and it would all be a bad nightmare.

The plane jostled him out of his gloomy thoughts as it taxied across the concourse. He was late. He should have arrived in Minoa two days earlier, but he'd been delayed by the ongoing investigation. Forced to spend extra time answering questions at the National Interagency Fire Center in Boise, Idaho. But he didn't mind. The media was hunting for him and he'd been grateful for the opportunity to avoid them. The news report he'd seen on TV last night indicated they'd done their research and knew the name of his hometown. Since he hadn't shown up in Minoa on schedule, they wouldn't know where he was. They'd be confused. Searching for him elsewhere. He hoped.

He sat quietly, gazing at the black asphalt. The plane came to a bumping stop. A few more minutes, and the attendant opened the door. Releasing his seat belt, Reese stood and flipped open the overhead bin. He shouldered his duffel bag, then stepped off the plane. He'd left this monotonous town as soon as he'd graduated from high school. The next day, to be exact. And he hadn't been home since. Eager for his freedom. Desperate to flee his father's drunken rages. The only thing he missed about this place was his mother. She'd taught him about God and how to pray, but it never seemed to take. He'd never cared about the Lord…until recently.

He looked around at the barren desert that budged up against the narrow airport strip. Clumps of sage and rabbitbrush covered the landscape, punctuated by an occasional piñon or juniper tree. Farther out, Cove Mountain stood like a sentinel guarding the valley below. The Western United States had been having a severe drought. With his practiced eye, Reese could tell the region was prime for another wildfire. All this area needed was a single strike of lightning or a careless camper for the place to go up in flames. And that thought terrified Reese. Because he didn't believe he could ever fight wildfires again. So what would he do to earn a living? He didn't have a clue. Fighting wildfires was all he knew. The only thing he'd ever been good at.

Adjusting the weight of his heavy pack, he headed toward the hangar. In an airport this size, there was only one building. Ed Hayden, the caretaker, should be inside. There were no taxis or rental cars in this town, so Reese had called ahead to ask for a lift. Ed had agreed to drive him into town. Otherwise, Reese would just hoof it. As a hotshot, he'd hiked many miles through rugged terrain that would leave most men gasping. He was in prime physical condition and the five-mile walk would be easy. The solitude might do him some good, too.

Inside the hangar, he passed by a forklift and another prop plane. The heavy smell of fuel made him crinkle his nose.

"Hello? Is anyone here?" He paused to listen for a moment.

No one responded. A scuffling noise came from behind him. He turned. A woman stood silhouetted in the doorway leading out to the parking lot. Although her face was in shadow, his guard went up like a kite flying high. The words *journalist* and *media* flashed across his brain. He was so weary of being hounded for an interview that he'd become cynical and wary. Surely the reporters were no longer expecting him. Ed had told him that several journalists had been by every day, waiting for him. He'd hoped when he hadn't shown up that they'd all left town.

The woman took a step into the sunlight. Dressed in a modest, flowered sundress and strappy sandals that accented her shapely ankles, she seemed vaguely familiar. His gaze shifted to her side. She held the hand of a little girl perhaps six years of age. He thought there was something familiar about the child, too. Something he couldn't quite put his finger on.

"Hello," the woman said, her voice low and strangely soothing.

"Hi, there," Reese returned, trying not to sound grouchy. Right now, he didn't want to talk to anyone but Ed Hayden.

"You look lost," she said.

"Nope. I'm just not sure where I'll be tomorrow, and that's not the same thing."

"Isn't it?" She tilted her head to one side. A spray of sunshine gleamed off her long auburn curls. Her lovely mouth curved in a slight smile that didn't quite reach her gentle brown eyes.

Yeah, he was sure he knew her, but what was her name? It was on the tip of his tongue, like the sweet taste of his mom's homemade sugar cookies.

The woman looked at him with an oddly penetrating gaze. As though she could see deep inside his blackened heart and knew every one of his failings. Every flaw. Every regret.

"You don't recognize me, do you?" she asked.

He took a deep, impatient breath through his nose. "Sure, I do."

But no, he didn't. And a flush of embarrassment heated his face. Right now, he needed to think what to do next. To go to his motel room and be left alone until he could figure out another career for himself. That was all he wanted.

She took a step closer and held out her hand. "I'm Kathleen Ashmore. You and I graduated from high school together."

Ah, yes. It all came flooding back like the rush of adrenaline when he was fighting fires. Katie Ashmore. But, boy! She'd changed. A lot. Gone was the plain, gawky girl with disorderly red hair, freckles, thick glasses and frumpy clothes. The class valedictorian. Her test scores had been off the charts. She'd had a scholarship to at least two Ivy League schools and wanted to be a pediatrician, as he recalled. So what was she doing here?

Reese blinked, stunned by her transition. Surely this couldn't be dreary little Katie Ashmore. No sirree. This woman had a gorgeous figure and delicate features any man would notice. She'd become a stunner in the looks department. The drab duckling had become an elegant swan. In fact, with her brains and beauty, he had no doubt she could do anything her heart desired.

"Of course I remember. You tutored me in math." He forced himself to relax. He smiled, wondering if she might give him a ride into town. He definitely wasn't eager to ask. The last thing he wanted was an old classmate hanging around him, asking questions about the wildfire and his crew.

"And science," she said.

"Yeah, right."

How could he forget? He'd been an athlete at their high school, with a scholarship to the University of Nevada in Reno. His mom had wanted him to study electrical engineering, but he didn't want to go to school. Not in those days. He'd longed to get away from his father. He'd always thought that work experience was as good as a formal education. So he'd chosen hotshot wildfire fighting. More action. More fun.

What a fool he'd been. Too stupid to recognize that hard work and determination would get him further ahead than partying with friends and sliding through life with a minimum of effort. He'd soon discovered that firefighting was intense, difficult work. But he'd come to love it. Until two weeks ago, he'd planned to work his way up and one day be promoted to superintendent. But things were different now. He no longer knew what he wanted.

The little girl with Katie was looking at him with a critical eye, as though she could see deep inside him. Again, he felt a familiarity with her that he didn't quite understand.

"You're the firefighter I saw on TV. The one that survived," the child said, her voice soft and matter-of-fact.

"Yeah," he said, a hard lump of sandpaper in his throat.

"I'm sorry you lost your friends," the kid said.

Reese couldn't detect a single ounce of guile in her voice. Her compassion seemed sincere. And coming from an innocent child, her words touched him like nothing else could.

"Yes, we were both sorry to hear about your hotshot crew. I'm glad you're okay," Katie said. Her expressive eyes crinkled at the corners, telling him she was genuinely concerned.

"Thanks, but I'd rather not talk about it," he said, trying not to sound too abrasive. After all, it wasn't their fault.

"I understand. Are you headed into town?" Katie asked.

"Yeah," he said, glancing around. Where was Ed?

During high school, Katie had tutored him a couple nights each week. He'd been smart enough, but he'd talked her into doing his homework and writing his research papers. She'd stared at him with doe-eyed adoration. He could have talked her into doing anything, and he had. He'd used her, taking her most precious gift. Now he felt guilty and embarrassed by it all. He'd been such an idiot. He never should have taken what belonged to her husband. He should have studied harder. Should have been kinder, more diligent and responsible.

"You used to wear glasses," he said.

She nodded. "I wear contact lenses now."

He paused, liking the change. "Are you home visiting your family?"

"No, I still live here," she said. "In fact, I never left town. I…I work for my father at his motel and also write articles for the *Minoa Daily News*."

Reese tensed. Another reporter. Just what he'd come here to avoid. But he couldn't figure out why she'd stayed in Minoa. Why she'd chosen to be a journalist for a shabby newspaper office when she could have gone to almost any college and studied biology or physics. Her father owned the Cowboy Country Inn, one of the two motels in town. In fact, Reese had made a reservation to stay there while he was visiting. But he couldn't envision this attractive woman cleaning rooms for a living.

He brushed past her. "Sorry, but I don't have a story for you."

"That's not why I'm here," she called to his retreating back.

He stopped. Turned. "Then what do you want?"

She hesitated. "This is Chrissy."

Standing behind the little girl, Katie rested her hands on the child's slender shoulders. Chrissy smiled, showing a tooth missing in front. She lifted a hand to wave, her long reddish-blond ponytail bouncing. Very cute. A smaller version of her mother. With startling green eyes.

Reese waved back impatiently. "Hi, there, Chrissy. Glad to meet you."

And he was. She was a child, after all. Looking at him with an open honesty and casual frankness that told him she didn't want anything from him. Probably the first person he'd met in the past two weeks that didn't want a news story, a special feature, or to know the details of what had happened to him. She just wanted to be friends. But the introduction didn't explain what Katie was doing here. Not that Reese cared. He'd rather not ask. It wasn't his business, after all.

"Do you need a ride?" Katie asked.

Since Ed still hadn't appeared, Reese released a pent-up breath and resigned himself to accepting her help. "I guess I do. Are you headed into town?"

"We are." She took Chrissy's hand and stepped out into the sunshine.

Reese followed as she walked toward a blue midsize hatchback parked nearby. At the vehicle, he paused.

"One thing, though," he said.

She opened the driver's door and helped Chrissy climb into the back seat. "And what's that?"

"No questions about the fire. I don't want to talk about it anymore. Not to anyone. Especially not a reporter." His voice sounded low and grumpy. He didn't mean to be so harsh, but he thought maybe it was for the best. He had to set some boundaries.

She frowned. “Okay, I got it.”

She turned to buckle Chrissy into her booster seat. Without asking, he tossed his duffel bag into the back and climbed into the passenger seat. Katie got in and started up the engine, put the car in gear and backed out of the parking place.

As they rode into town, he gazed at her pretty profile. She stared out the windshield, her shoulders squared, her delicate hands gripping the steering wheel like a lifeline. Just two weeks ago, he might have thought about asking her out on a date. But right now, all he wanted was to be left alone.

He was watching her. Katie could feel Reese’s eyes on her as she headed out onto the county road that would take them into town. A glint of sunlight struck the black asphalt. Momentarily blinded, she blinked and tried to ignore the man sitting so close beside her. Trying to remember why she’d come here in the first place.

Focus! she told herself. She mustn’t forget that her main priority was Chrissy, not a drop-dead-gorgeous hunk from her past. Until last night, she hadn’t been sure that Reese would come home. Not until her father had told her about his motel reservation. He knew she needed to speak with Reese in a place where there weren’t lots of people around. Not many flights came into the quiet airport, so it was easy to find out when he might be landing.

Thinking he might need a ride, she’d driven out here to pick him up. But nothing had prepared her to see him again. The shock. The resentment. The longing. Those feelings were still tied up inside her stomach like knots of rope.

There'd been a time during high school when she would have given anything to have him notice her. Back then, she'd been happy to do his homework. Delighted that he needed her for something. She'd loved him from afar, hungering for his attention. A girlhood crush. And when his date at the graduation dance had flirted with another boy, they'd quarreled. In retaliation, Reese had taken Katie's hand and pulled her outside the school gymnasium with him. Katie had known he was trying to make his girlfriend jealous, but she'd gone along willingly, euphoric when he'd kissed her in the dark shadows. At the time, she hadn't cared about his reasons or the consequences. But his affection had been short-lived. The very next day, she'd learned that he'd left town without even saying goodbye to his mom. Katie had sold herself short, but never again. Now she had a child to raise, and Chrissy was everything to her.

"Can I turn on the air?" he asked.

She nodded. "Of course."

He reached out and twisted a knob on the dashboard, hiking the air conditioner to high. The whooshing sound seemed to taunt her.

She glanced at Reese, longing to study the subtle changes to his face. She hadn't seen him in seven years. Gone was the teenage kid she'd known in high school. Now he was a fully matured man. Shockingly handsome, with short dark hair and an endearing half smile that still had the power to melt her frozen heart. He'd filled out more, his chest and shoulders wider and more muscular. He had big hands and quiet eyes. As though he were keeping a dark secret hidden from the entire world.

His eyes also held a glint of insecurity and deep, wrenching grief. He seemed to have lost his way, which couldn't be true. Reese Hartnett had always been so self-assured. Living in the moment. Louder and bigger than life. Never caring about anything or anyone. And Katie hated that she had loved him once. Hated that she was compelled to come and see him now. No matter how much she regretted the past, it was finally time to tell him the truth.

"How long are you in town for?" she asked, forcing herself to focus on the road ahead. His reservation at the motel was "open," which meant he had no scheduled departure date.

He jerked a shoulder. "That depends."

"On what?"

"On how many questions people ask. I'm hoping everyone just leaves me alone."

"Oh," she said, feeling a bit hurt and offended at the same time. "Well, I suppose your old friends will want to talk to you, to find out where you've been and what you've been up to."

"My friends are all gone now," he said.

She thought he was teasing, but the look on his face told her he was serious. He'd gone pale and a flash of pain filled his eyes. She couldn't think of one old friend of Reese's who hadn't been wilder than a March hare. Most of them had left town, which could be a blessing. She hated the thought of him falling back in with a rough crowd. But right now, she thought he was probably talking about his hotshot crew.

"Losing both of your parents and now your team members must have been difficult for you. I'm sorry for your loss," she said.

He didn't respond, and she adjusted the flow of the vent and took a gulping breath of fresh air. They entered town and she drove down Main Street. Reese sat up straighter, but he pulled a baseball cap out of his back pocket and tugged it low over his forehead as he looked out the window with interest. They passed the Rocklin Diner, the only restaurant in town. The two grocery stores still sat facing each other on either side of the street, and then the redbrick bank and post office.

Reese released a long sigh. "I see that nothing has changed."

"Not much," Katie agreed.

Except for maybe the two of them.

"We got a new swimming pool last summer, over by the high school," Chrissy said.

"That's right. It's real nice. You'll have to try it out sometime," Katie said.

Reese nodded but didn't comment.

"We don't go to the pool in town. We've got our own pool at the motel. Mommy's teaching me to swim," Chrissy continued, her voice filled with delight.

"Is that right?" Reese asked in a conversational tone.

"Yep, and I'm getting good at it. I can float on my back all by myself and even duck my head under without getting water up my nose," Chrissy said.

"That's nice." Reese flashed a brooding smile that used to turn Katie's brains to mush. But no more. No, sirree. She was over this guy.

He glanced at Katie. "Who did you marry? Anyone I know?"

Here it was. She hadn't expected to talk about such personal things so soon. She took a deep breath and let it out slowly. Before she could respond, Chrissy answered for her.

"Mommy's not married." The girl sat forward, her expression innocent.

He quirked one eyebrow at the child. "She's not, huh?"

He shifted his gaze over to Katie. “Are you divorced, then?”

A fist of emotion clogged her throat. Her face felt flushed with heat. And once again, that old crushing anger filled her. Anger because Reese had used her, then cast her aside. She’d meant so little to him. And yet it was not entirely fair to be upset at him for something he didn’t even know about. She was mostly angry at herself for getting herself into trouble. For ever trusting him.

“I’d rather not talk about it,” she said.

His eyebrows spiked.

“Mommy’s never been married,” Chrissy supplied.

Katie flinched. Maybe she shouldn’t have brought her daughter along on this visit. Maybe she should have met with Reese in private first. But she’d wanted to see how he acted around the child before telling him that he was Chrissy’s daddy.

“Sit back and put your seat belt back on, young lady.” She gave her daughter a stern look in the rearview mirror.

Chrissy pursed her lips but sat back obediently in her booster seat and reclicked the belt into place.

Reese hesitated, the corners of his eyes crinkling, so that Katie thought he might smile. But he didn’t.

“Sorry. I didn’t mean to pry,” he said.

Katie held her breath for several moments, forcing herself not to blurt it all out. He’d assumed because she had a child that she was married.

“I understand you’re staying tonight at the Cowboy Country Inn. Do you want me to take you straight there, or somewhere else?” Katie asked, glad to change the subject.

She’d come here with the single purpose of speaking the truth, but something held her back. After all, she wasn’t sure what to expect once Reese found out that Chrissy was his daughter. For all Katie knew, he might yell and scream and start throwing things. She didn't want Chrissy subjected to anything unpleasant. It would be best if the little girl wasn't present when she told Reese.

"Just take me to your inn. I figured it would be the best place for me to stay. Is Rigbee's Motel still a dive?" he asked, a slight smile curving his handsome mouth. Was he teasing her?

"Oh, no, it's a real nice place now. The bedbugs come at no extra charge," Katie quipped.

His vivid green eyes were tinged by a bit of reckless laughter. "In that case, I'm glad I chose the Cowboy Country Inn."

"Yes, my dad told me you'd made a reservation. Our rooms are always clean and comfortable," Katie said.

"Does Rigbee's have bedbugs?" Chrissy asked from the back seat.

Looking in the rearview mirror, Katie saw that her daughter's expressive green eyes were round with disbelief. Eyes that looked so much like her father's. Living in a motel, the little girl had heard all about bedbugs and cleanliness standards. It was their family business, after all.

"No, honey. We're just joking," Katie said.

"Because they're our competition?" the girl asked.

"Yes, honey," Katie said.

"Or maybe not," Reese mumbled under his breath.

Katie chuckled as she turned the corner and headed toward home. "We've had a lot of reporters staying at our place."

A flash of panic filled Reese's eyes and his back stiffened.

"Don't worry," she said. "When you didn't show up

earlier this week, they all checked out this morning. I'm sure they've left town by now."

She hoped. The pushy journalists and their cameramen had been a nuisance in their quiet town. Incessant questions about Reese and listening in on private conversations. She'd found one man hiding behind the ice machine. He'd given her the willies.

Reese relaxed as she pulled into the parking lot. Katie loved the old motel where she'd grown up and was now raising her own child. It wasn't fancy, but it was clean and well maintained. And in that moment, Katie thought she was crazy to have gone to the airport to pick up Reese. Her life was boring and lonely, but at least she and her daughter were secure here.

What must she have been thinking? She'd kept her daughter's paternity a secret for all these years, telling no one except her parents. Now that her mom was gone, only her dad knew the truth.

Two weeks ago, Katie had heard on the national news that Reese had lost his entire hotshot crew. And knowing that he'd almost died had changed something inside her.

Ever since she'd started kindergarten, Chrissy had been asking questions about her father. Why the other kids at school had a dad, but she didn't. Why he never came to her dance recitals, or took her to the park. Katie had been surprised that her daughter missed her father's presence in her life, even though Papa Charlie was always there. And that had made Katie realize it wasn't fair for Chrissy to never meet her dad. To never know who he was. For good or bad, the girl had a right to know. So Katie had decided to tell Reese. But she had to proceed with caution. She had a lot to lose.

Within moments, they pulled into a parking spot. A

long row of quaint, freshly painted doors sprawled out before them. A large, old-fashioned buckboard wagon sat near the main office, its side painted bright red, with the name of the motel written across it in tidy black letters. Antique milk cans filled with bright pink petunias stood like sentinels along the paved walkway leading to the front entrance. Charming and attractive. A homey place to stay.

"Here we are," Katie said.

"It still looks the same. The milk cans are new," Reese said.

"Yes, we put them in a couple of years ago."

"I helped Mommy plant the flowers yesterday," Chrissy chimed in.

"You did, huh? They look real nice." Reese spoke in a kind tone and the child beamed happily.

Katie opened her door and hopped out, suddenly eager to get away from this man she could neither forgive nor forget. She needed time to think. Now that Reese and Chrissy had met, she had to plan how to tell him. She'd wait until Chrissy wasn't around and find the right moment.

Turning, Katie reached into the back to help the little girl out of her booster seat. Reese popped his seat belt and stepped out, too, then lifted his duffel bag from the rear.

"Come to the office and Charlie will get you checked in," Katie called.

Without waiting for his acknowledgment, she headed in that direction, forcing herself not to look back to see if he followed. He did. Like the pull of a magnet, she could feel him behind her, his gaze seeming to drill a hole through her spine.

She wasn't sure she wanted him staying at the Cowboy Country Inn, but maybe it was for the best. Katie had to figure this out. But no matter what, she knew that telling him the truth would be the hardest thing she'd done yet. And once she did, nothing would ever be the same again.

Chapter Two

"Did you tell him?"

Katie dropped the mechanical pencil she'd been holding. It hit the computer keyboard and bounced onto the floor. Swiveling around, she picked it up, then sat back and stared at her father. Charlie Ashmore stood in the open doorway to the motel office, gripping his walking cane with one hand.

"Dad..." She spoke in an annoyed tone, hoping he'd take the hint and leave her alone. But he didn't budge.

"I'd like to know. I don't want to accidentally say something I shouldn't while he's staying here," he said.

Katie chose to ignore his comments. "Did you get him situated in a room?"

"Yes. Milly took him some extra towels and a key to the pool. He walked down to Rocklin Diner to get something to eat."

The restaurant was six blocks away. Maybe Katie should have offered Reese some lunch, but her mind was swirling with emotions. She told herself that she didn't want him here. But deep in her heart, she was glad to see him again, grateful that he hadn't died in the wildfire that had killed his crew. She refused to consider why she cared. Surely it was just because he was Chrissy's father. Somehow, she knew it was something more. Something she couldn't explain even after all these years.

"Maybe it's not a good idea for him to stay here," she said.

Charlie shrugged. "Why not? I know how difficult this situation is for you, but it was inevitable that he would come home for a visit someday. Besides, where else was he going to stay?"

He didn't mention Rigbee's Motel. He didn't have to. It wasn't a joke that they'd been accused of having bed-bugs. Knowing her father was right didn't make her feel any better.

"Where's Chrissy?" Katie asked.

"In the living room watching TV."

The living room. A large suite of rooms they'd converted for their own use. It included a soft sofa, two recliners, a bookshelf and a wide flat-screen TV. It wasn't fancy, but it was clean and comfy, and they were happy, most of the time. With a few maids to clean the rooms, Charlie oversaw the front reception desk, while Katie did the books. They made a good team, running the Cowboy Country Inn together. But just now, Charlie's mouth was stretched into a straight, solemn line that made his white mustache twitch.

"Did you tell him?" he asked again.

Katie's gaze clashed with her father's. "No, I didn't."

"Why not?" he persisted.

She looked away, an impatient sigh squeezing from her lungs. "I couldn't tell him with Chrissy sitting there listening in."

"You could have left her home with me," he suggested.

She shook her head. "No, I wanted to see them together first. I want to proceed with caution. Telling him might be a mistake."

"Why?"

"What if he causes trouble?"

Charlie shook his head. "I don't think Reese is the type of man to do that. Not about his own child."

She didn't think so, either, but she wasn't sure. After all, he was a fully grown man now, and she knew nothing about him. How he'd been living his life. If he was married or divorced. If he had other children somewhere. Nothing.

"He wasn't a very nice person in high school," she said.

"With his background, can you blame him?" Charlie asked.

"What do you mean?"

"Have you forgotten about his father?"

She crinkled her eyebrows. "No, I remember."

Everyone had known Hank Hartnett. Passed out in the middle of the sidewalk. Causing a brawl in the bank when his account was overdrawn. The bruises on his wife's face. And sometimes on Reese's face, too. The man was a constant source of gossip. The town drunk.

"But that doesn't excuse Reese's actions. We don't know him anymore. What if he takes me to court? He might try to take Chrissy away and then what would I do?" Katie met her father's gaze, trying to keep the fear she was feeling from showing in her eyes.

Charlie's stiff demeanor softened as he limped over to the desk and squeezed her arm. "Ah, honey. You're worrying too much about this. I don't think Reese would do something like that. Right now, I think he's hurting. He just needs a place to lie low, where he can receive some kindness and understanding."

Katie brushed a hand across her forehead, trying to

keep her composure. She didn't like this situation. Not one bit.

Charlie sat on a corner of the desk, one gnarled hand resting in his lap. "I looked into his eyes. He's still got a lot of kindness there. Did I ever tell you about the time I saw some of his friends picking on a stray dog?"

"No," she said.

"The poor animal looked scrawny and half-starved. Reese was only about ten years old at the time. His friends were throwing rocks and hitting the dog with a stick. Reese got so angry at them. He defended the dog. In fact, he took the animal home with him. Next thing I knew, his mom was down in town buying dog food. And you know what he named that mangy old mutt?"

She shook her ahead.

"Duke. He treated that dog like royalty. I saw them together a few months later and couldn't believe the transition. Duke had filled out and looked happy and healthy. He followed that boy everywhere, completely devoted to him."

Katie didn't really care about a stray dog right now. "And your point is?"

"My point is that there's goodness inside of Reese. I've seen it. His mom attended church every Sunday, fighting to keep her family together. She had to be a remarkable lady to stay with that no-good husband of hers. But I have no doubt her teachings rubbed off on Reese, whether he liked it or not. It's still there inside of him. He just has to let it come out."

Katie snorted. "I doubt that's going to happen."

"Why don't we give him the benefit of the doubt?" Charlie suggested.

She pursed her lips and turned back to her work, trying to focus on the computer monitor. The electronic spreadsheet swam before her eyes, the numbers a blurry haze. She'd been working on the ledgers for over an hour and had accomplished nothing. Finally. Finally, she could tell Reese exactly what she thought of him. And yet words failed her somehow.

She glanced at her father, feeling annoyed. "This isn't a simple matter, Dad."

"Ah, honey. You take things way too seriously. Can't you forgive him? After all, he doesn't even know he has a child," Charlie said.

True. And that left Katie feeling a tad guilty.

"Maybe if he hadn't left town so fast, I could have told him I was pregnant," she said.

"You could have tracked him down," Charlie pointed out.

She jerked her head up. "How? Even his mom didn't know where he'd gone. I asked. She was brokenhearted. It was horrible for him to leave the way he did. No forwarding address. No way to find him."

Charlie folded his arms and gazed at her quietly. "Are we talking about how he left his parents, or how he left you?"

She blinked, wanting to cry. Wanting to scream and kick and yell. It had hurt her so deeply when she'd found out Reese was gone. It was obvious that their one time together had meant a lot more to her than it had to him. Of course, he'd been drinking heavily that night. Maybe he didn't even remember what had happened between them. But she did. She could never forget.

Charlie quirked one bushy eyebrow. "I know you'll tell him when the time is right."

Maybe. Maybe not.

She tried to forget the past, but it wasn't easy. Overnight, her full-ride scholarship had been flushed down the tubes. It wouldn't pay for diapers and childcare. And giving her baby up for adoption wasn't an option for her. So she'd stayed here in Minoa to raise her child. Without a husband. Living in a town where she'd become a pariah. No one wanted to date her. No one knew who Chrissy's father was. For years, Katie had kept the gossip mill busy. And now Reese had walked back into her life.

A crash came from outside in the parking lot, as though someone had tipped over a large garbage can. Both Katie and Charlie whirled around. Someone yelled and then a low roar of voices permeated the small office.

"What on earth is that?" Charlie said.

Chrissy came running into the room, her eyes wide with fear, her little chin quivering. "Mommy! There's a strange man looking in my window."

At that precise moment, a man's face appeared at the window in the office. Cupping his hands around his eyes to shut out the sunlight, he peered inside.

"Hey! There's someone in here," he yelled.

A large black camera lifted toward them, its red light blinking. And in an instant, Katie understood. Somehow, the media had found out that Reese was staying here.

"That does it," Charlie said. "Call 9-1-1 and tell the police we're being swarmed by reporters."

"Reporters?" Chrissy said.

"Yeah, I figured it was just a matter of time before this happened, but I thought Reese would be safe for a day or two. Call the police." Charlie limped toward the door, his jaw hard.

Turning toward the desk, Katie reached for the phone. As she dialed the numbers, she couldn't help wondering where Reese was and what might happen next.

Reese heard the cacophony before he saw the myriad of people milling around the parking lot at the Cowboy Country Inn. He'd been hungry, so he'd walked the short distance to the Rocklin Diner and gotten a sandwich. Wearing a baseball cap pulled low across his face, he'd escaped recognition. No questions to answer. No big deal. Now he was beat. He hadn't been sleeping well and longed to lie down and close his eyes for a million years.

"There he is!" someone yelled.

Reese lifted his head and paused. A small crowd of people stood in the parking lot of the motel. With a glance, he took in two camera crews and reporters running straight toward him. A news van with *Channel 6* written on the side was parked directly in front of his room. A woman gripping a microphone in one hand pounded on his door. How had they found out which room he was staying in? Surely Katie or Charlie wouldn't tell them.

For two brief moments, Reese thought about making a run for it. His hesitation cost him dearly. The swarm came at him like a trampling herd. He found himself surrounded, the reporters thrusting their mics into his face. The flash of cameras caused him to blink.

"Mr. Hartnett, can you tell us about the last few minutes before your hotshot crew died?" one of them asked, holding a recorder in front of his nose.

"How did it happen, Reese? How did it make you feel?" another one said.

They packed closer, vying for his attention. Reese felt the blood drain from his face. He tensed, his body cold and shaking. His stomach churned. This was exactly what he'd tried to avoid: a media frenzy. He wasn't about to discuss his personal feelings with anyone. In fact, he'd rather forget the incident ever happened.

"Break it up. You're on private property. I want you all to leave." Gripping his wooden cane, Charlie Ashmore pushed his way into the group, a deep scowl pulling at his eyebrows.

The reporters ignored Charlie, jostling him so that he stumbled. Reese snatched the man's arm to steady him. "Are you okay?"

Charlie met his gaze and nodded.

"What was it like, watching your crew die like that?" someone asked.

Reese shuddered as memories sliced over him like slivers of ice. His ears rang with the screams of dying men.

"You have no right to ask him such personal things. You need to leave right now." Katie came out of the motel, brandishing a broom like a warrior. Chrissy stood close beside her mother, her eyes wide.

Katie took a sweep at two of the reporters' legs and they jumped back. Anger flared across her face, her long auburn hair whipping about her shoulders like a flame. She was absolutely gorgeous in her fury.

"You get out of here, all of you," she ordered.

"We don't mean any harm. We're just after a story," one of the journalists said.

"I don't care what you're after. You need to leave. I've just called the police," she said, throttling the broomstick with her hands.

Confusion fogged Reese's brain. Katie was defending him? He couldn't believe it. They'd been friends in high school. Sort of. Not really. But that was a long time ago. And he admitted silently that he'd never treated Katie very well. He'd been pretty drunk the night of their graduation when he'd used her abominably. He barely remembered the details, but he still knew what he'd done. So why was she standing up for him now?

"Look, I don't want any trouble. I have nothing to say.

There's no story here, so you might as well leave." Reese spoke above the dull roar.

He held up his hands, as if to ward them off. Like a wolf scenting blood, they moved in closer.

"You heard him, folks. You need to pack it up and go home," Charlie boomed. Lifting his cane, he used it to push his way through the throng.

Reese made a break for it but found his path blocked by a short, stocky man holding a digital recorder. "What does it feel like to be the only one who survived?"

Bruce Miller. Reese recognized the award-winning reporter immediately. He was with the National News Registry. Headstrong, assertive and unwilling to take no for an answer. Bruce had been dogging Reese for two weeks. When he wasn't carrying on an interview, he held a plump, stinky cigar clenched between his teeth. The guy was relentless.

In the jostling crowd, Charlie bumped against Bruce. "I asked you to leave."

"You don't have to be so pushy about it." Bruce glared his disapproval.

A shrill siren sounded, growing louder as a squad car pulled into the parking lot. Tilting his head to one side, Reese breathed an audible sigh of relief. With the police here, Katie leaned her broom against the outer wall and stood with Chrissy beside the office door. Her cheeks were a pretty shade of pink, her eyes crinkled with concern. For him. No, surely he imagined that. She was just worried about all the people standing in the parking lot of her motel. It was bad for business, after all.

Reese gravitated toward her, grateful to see a familiar face. Right now, he felt adrift in a stormy sea of doubt, with multiple leaks in his life raft. She was like a lifeline, reeling him in. For the first time in a long time, he needed someone else's help, and that left him feeling strangely humbled.

"What's going on here?" Martin Sanders, the chief of police, got out of his squad car and strode toward the mob.

Reese hesitated. As a teenager, he'd had plenty of altercations with this officer. So had his father. Reese couldn't remember the number of times his dad had been locked in a cell overnight for being drunk and disorderly or writing a bad check. Either Reese or his mom had always bailed him out. Most of the money Reese made working summer jobs had been taken by his dad to buy booze. Instead of buying new school clothes, Reese's mom had let out the hems in his old pants and mended his threadbare socks and shirts. Being poor because of his father's penchant for drink had taken its toll on Reese's morale. He hated being the child of a drunkard.

Chief Sanders looked older now, with gray at his temples, but he was still big, tall and capable. He tugged up his duty belt, laden with a gun, handcuffs and a Taser. It was obvious from his fierce demeanor that he knew how to handle himself with these reporters.

"Thanks for coming, Chief Sanders. I've asked them all to leave, but they've refused," Charlie said.

"What's the big deal? We just want an interview," Bruce Miller called.

Sanders turned and looked at Reese. "Are you the cause of all this ruckus?"

Reese nodded. "Yes, sir, but I don't mean any harm."

As the policeman sized him up, recognition flashed in his eyes, followed by a glaze of distaste. Reese couldn't blame him. No doubt the lawman remembered every rotten act he'd committed when he was a youth. Destroying property, tagging fences with spray paint, getting drunk with his friends. In retrospect, Reese didn't know why he'd done such things. It was as if he'd wanted to get back at his father for all the pain he caused at home.

"Do you want to give them an interview?" Sanders asked.

Reese shook his head. "No, sir. I have nothing to say to any of them."

A thought occurred to him and he suddenly knew how they'd found him. Over an hour earlier, Milly Carver had delivered extra towels to his room before he went to lunch. No doubt the maid had blabbed that he was here and news had spread like wildfire.

Sanders faced the crowd. "You heard him, folks. You'll have to leave now. Most of you are from out of town. I suggest you get in your cars and keep on going."

"I'd like another room here for the night," Bruce said.

"Sorry, but since you checked out this morning, I have no rooms available for any of you," Charlie said.

Reese hated to be the cause of the man losing business.

"If you take the main road into Carson City, I'm sure you'll find accommodations there, or in Reno. Or you can stay at Rigbee's Motel down the street," Charlie said.

"Yeah, sure," Bruce groused.

They all grumbled but slowly drifted away, leaving Reese in peace.

"Take him inside the office." Charlie nudged Katie, but she didn't move, seeming frozen in place.

"Come on. Follow me."

Reese looked down and found Chrissy holding his hand. Locking her jaw and lifting her chin with determination, she led him into the relative safety of the reception room. There was something familiar about the way she tilted her head, but he couldn't figure it out. Nor did he understand why this child and her mother were trying to protect him. He wasn't used to being rescued.

Inside the office, Reese breathed a sigh of relief. He could still hear the reporters outside and Chief Sanders's booming voice as he directed them to pack up their equipment. Maybe Reese should leave town, but he hadn't gone to the cemetery to visit his mom yet. He wanted to stay at least long enough to pay his respects to her. So, what should he do? Where could he go?

"Thanks for that," he said to Charlie and Katie. Highly conscious that Chrissy was still gripping his hand, he politely withdrew.

"They'll just come back. What can we do?" Katie asked her father.

Charlie shrugged. "He'll have to leave, of course."

"But where will he go?" she said.

Reese chuckled. "You know, I'm right here. You don't need to talk as though I'm not listening to your conversation."

Katie licked her bottom lip. "I'm sorry, Reese. I'm just concerned, that's all. I don't want trouble."

"Neither do I," he said.

"What do you want to do, then?" she asked.

"You're right. I can't stay here, that's for sure," he stated.

"Don't be sad," Chrissy said. "Mommy says that things always have a way of working themselves out. We just need to have faith."

"Yeah, thanks." Reese gave a stiff smile.

He couldn't believe that this little girl was trying to comfort him. He found the child endearing, but her clinging presence also made him uncomfortable. He didn't know why she seemed to like him so much.

"What about Cove Mountain?" Charlie asked.

Katie glanced at her father, her eyebrows drawn together in a frown. "Are you sure?"

"Of course," Charlie said. "It's a great place to hide out. It's rugged and isolated enough that most reporters would get lost trying to find it. Without four-wheel drive, their cars would bottom out on the washboard roads and they'd end up with a broken axel."

"Cove Mountain? You mean your cabin up there?" Reese said.

He recalled that the Ashmores had a log cabin in the lovely mountains surrounding the town. Reese had been there a few times with his Boy Scout troop, before he'd become too wild to enjoy fishing and hiking. The times he'd been there had been idyllic. That was when he'd decided that he wanted to fight wildfires. About twenty miles outside town, the three-room cabin was tucked back in a forest surrounded by tall Douglas fir and pine trees.

"Yes, our cabin. You'll go to Cove Mountain," Charlie said with finality.

"Are you sure you want to do that?" Reese asked, conscious of little Chrissy listening intently to every word.

"I am," Charlie said. "If we're careful, no one will discover you. Katie can take you in the back way. There's no cell phone service, but Martha Murdoch lives near the cabin and she has a landline you can use in an emergency. She'll notice smoke coming from the chimney, but she'll think it's us. Even if she finds out you're staying there, she hates gossip and won't bother you."

"That sounds fine. I'll pay you rent," Reese said.

Charlie shook his head. "That's not necessary. It's too rustic for us to charge a fee."

"Why are you helping me?" Reese asked. He could

hardly believe this generosity. After all, he'd done nothing to deserve it.

"Because you're a Minoa boy, and we take care of our own," Charlie said.

Once again, Reese was touched by this family's kindness toward him. He had no idea how he could ever make it up to them.

"Thank you," he said.

Speaking those words felt good. Mainly because it'd been a very long time since he'd said them to anyone.

"You're welcome." Charlie reached into a desk drawer and pulled out a set of keys, which he handed to Reese. "Katie will drive you up there. It's a pretty deserted road."

"Come on, let's get going," Katie said, her frown still firmly in place.

"I want to go, too," Chrissy said.

"Not this time, bug. I need you to stay here and help me watch the front desk." Charlie reached down and tickled the girl's ribs.

Chrissy giggled and swatted playfully at her grandpa's hand. "You don't need me, Papa. I want to go with Mommy and Reese."

"Not this time, sweetie," he insisted firmly.

Katie met her father's gaze. A flash of doubt filled her eyes and she looked away with a slight huff. Reese couldn't be sure, but he sensed that Charlie had purposefully set Katie up so that she could be alone with him during the ride to the cabin. Nah! Surely he imagined that. What possible reason would Charlie have for them to be alone?

Turning, Reese followed Katie out the back door, watching her closely. The years had been kind to her and he couldn't get over how gorgeous she was.

"Let me grab my things," he said.

She nodded and he peeked outside the office. No media in sight. Chief Sanders had done his job.

Reese took the opportunity to quickly race to his room, snatch up his duffel bag and return to the office. He laid his room key on the counter.

Charlie smiled. “See you later.”

“Yeah, later,” Reese said.

Katie led him out the door to the alleyway. She looked back and forth, to ensure no one was there to watch them slip inside the garage. As she climbed into the driver’s seat of her father’s old truck and started up the engine, Reese felt suddenly light of heart. He was glad to get away from the crush of media. For some insane reason, he felt safe with this woman and her family. But if the stern set of Katie’s shoulders and the deep frown curving her lips were any indication, Reese didn’t think she returned the sentiment. She disapproved of him, just as he disapproved of himself.

Chapter Three

"You sure pack light," Katie said.

She shifted the truck into gear and eyed Reese's duffel bag, which sat between them on the seat. Pulling out of the garage, she looked both ways, hoping to avoid being seen. She headed out on the old dirt road that would lead them to the outskirts of town and up toward Cove Mountain.

"I don't need much." Reese spoke in a subdued tone.

She took a deep inhalation and caught his spicy scent. The truck bounced against the rutted road. They drove in silence for some time, passing a green meadow of new grass and blue lupines. Tall willow trees swayed gently in the breeze.

"I'm surprised you stayed here in Minoa all these years. I thought you were planning to go to college," Reese said.

"I was." She couldn't look at him. Sudden tears burned her eyes and she blinked fast to clear them away. A gloomy, lost sensation enveloped her. She thought she'd gotten over feeling sorry for herself. So why the unexpected emotion?

"You must have had Chrissy pretty young. Is she why you stayed?" he asked.

"Um, yeah," Katie said.

The road climbed steadily in elevation, the terrain becoming rocky, the piñons and junipers giving way to tall evergreens.

"Why couldn't you take her with you?"

When she didn't answer, he looked at her. A flush of anger heated her skin. She didn't owe this man any explanations. Not without blurting the entire story of how he'd left her pregnant at the tender age of seventeen, and she'd been completely dependent upon her parents for financial and emotional support. Barely out of high school. No job. No way to support herself and her unborn child.

She had to tell him. Her faith in God had sustained her through the long, lonely years, but she wasn't feeling too generous toward Reese at the moment. She doubted this wound would ever heal.

"I noticed your mom's not around anymore. Did something happen to her?" Reese asked in a kind tone.

A deep sadness swept over her. "Cancer. She died early last year."

"I'm sorry to hear that. She was a nice lady."

She glanced at Reese, his comment taking her off guard. She wasn't used to this gentle side of him and wondered if he really meant it. His profile looked strong and handsome, yet forlorn in a remote sort of way. His beautiful green eyes no longer sparkled with a zest for life, but his words seemed genuine enough.

"I'll bet she loved Chrissy," he said.

Katie tightened her hands around the steering wheel. "Yes, she did."

"She's a nice kid. Really cute," he said.

Tell him. Tell him now.

"She should be. She's yours." Katie blurted the words before she could take them back. She wondered if she'd regret it, but then she felt a modicum of peace.

Finally. Finally, she'd told him the truth and unloaded the burden from her heart. For good or bad, the secret was out now, and the prospects both relieved and terrified her.

He jerked his head toward her, his eyebrows drawn together in a quizzical frown. "What did you say?"

Katie's heart pounded and she breathed fast through her mouth as she pulled up in front of the log cabin. Charlie had built it with his own hands before Katie was even born. It wasn't large, just three rooms, but it was tidy and comfortable. A sparkling creek ran parallel to the property. The lake was three miles farther down the road. Her family had frequently spent weekends up here, fishing, hiking, sharing sweet memories. But lately, Chrissy kept mentioning that she wished her dad would go fishing with her.

Katie pulled into the graveled driveway and shut off the engine. Clenching her hands together in her lap, she stared straight ahead. "You heard me correctly. You are Chrissy's father."

"When? How?" he asked, his razor-sharp gaze narrowed on her face.

"You know when. You know how," she said, hoping he wouldn't accuse her of lying. She'd never been with anyone else. Since the night they'd graduated from high school, she'd gone out on a couple dates, but no one was interested in getting tied up with her excess baggage—an adorable little girl named Chrissy.

"How…how old is your daughter?" he asked.

Your daughter.

Funny how he refused to claim Chrissy as his own. That could be good or bad, depending on what happened next. A wave of fear washed over Katie. What if he tried to take Chrissy away from her? Or what if he wanted nothing to do with the child, just like he'd wanted nothing to do with her? She would never let Reese hurt Chrissy. Not if she could help it.

"She's just over six years old. You do the math." Katie tried desperately to speak in an even tone.

"What's her birthday?" he asked.

"March 4. I delivered a week late, which is normal for a first-time mother," she responded without hesitation.

She could almost see his mental calculations clicking away. They'd graduated from high school on June 6. According to Reese's mother, he'd left town on June 7. Chrissy was born almost exactly nine months later.

"I'm her father?" He blinked, as though he couldn't believe it.

"Yes. Your name is on her birth certificate."

Katie could imagine how he was feeling. Shocked. Confused. The same way she'd felt when she'd found out she was pregnant out of wedlock. In a larger community, no one would care. But in sleepy Minoa, many people didn't approve. She told herself that she didn't care what Reese or anyone else thought. Her child was all that mattered. And yet Katie knew that wasn't true. She'd cared deeply about Reese all those years ago. Her heart had wrenched when she'd thought about him being killed two weeks earlier, in the wildfire that had engulfed his hotshot crew. But that didn't mean she still loved him. She was just concerned for his welfare, nothing more.

He paused for a few moments, as if he were thinking this through. "Why didn't you tell me I had a daughter?"

She snorted and whirled on him. "How could I? By the time I found out I was pregnant, you were long gone. No one knew where you went. Not even your mom."

He raked his fingers through his short, dark hair and blew out a harsh breath. "Did my folks know about Chrissy?"

"They knew I had her, but they never knew you were her father. I've never told anyone, except my mom and dad. But I saw your parents around town from time to time and they always doted on Chrissy. Even your father. He thought she was the cutest baby he'd ever seen, next to you."

Reese jerked his head up. "He actually said that?"

Katie nodded.

He scoffed with disbelief. "I doubt my dad was sober enough to understand even if you had told him the truth."

She agreed. The man was always drunk. And from the gossip she'd heard, he was a mean drunk. Living with such a man couldn't have been easy on Reese or his mother. And yet the few times Hank Hartnett had seen Chrissy, when they were downtown in the grocery store, he'd smiled and played with the baby so sweetly. Obviously he had a good side, but maybe Reese had never seen that part of him.

"Your mom gave me a beautiful baby afghan she knitted when Chrissy was born. It's made of soft yellow yarn. I've kept it safe so it wouldn't get bedraggled. I thought Chrissy might like to have it when she's old enough to understand who her other grandma was. I asked your mom where you had gone, but she said she didn't know. I could see in her eyes that she was heartbroken that you'd left like that."

He clenched his eyes shut, his mouth tight. Katie could tell that her words pained him, but he needed to hear the truth. He needed to understand what he'd left behind for all of them to cope with.

"I didn't feel like there was anything for me here in Minoa." His voice sounded soft and hoarse.

His words hurt so much. She'd been nothing more than a one-night stand. A fling. Certainly nothing lasting. And she'd been left to pick up the pieces without him.

"What about your mom?" Katie asked, wondering how he could just abandon the woman to his father's drunken rages.

"I pleaded with her to go with me, but she refused. She wouldn't leave my dad. About a year after I got settled on a fire crew, I called her a couple of times and told her where I was, but she just cried and asked me to come home. I knew that would never work, so I stopped calling."

A long, swelling silence filled the air. His words caused a shudder to sweep down Katie's spine. She'd asked his mother about him only a couple of times. After the first year, she'd stopped asking. She could only wonder how bad his home life must have been. But he hesitated, as if there was something else he wanted to say. Something important. But he must have changed his mind, because he shrugged it off.

"So, you named her Chrissy?" he asked.

Katie nodded, wiping her damp eyes. "Yes. Christine Joy."

He jerked his head up. "Joy is her middle name?"

"Yes."

A half smile curved his handsome lips. "That was my mother's name."

"That's right. And Christine was my mom's name."

"You named our child after our two mothers." It was a statement, not a question.

Our child.

The words left Katie trembling. She wasn't sure that

she wanted to share Chrissy with him. She'd been raising her daughter on her own for so long that she didn't know if she wanted to include him in the mix. But now it was too late. Whether she liked it or not, she'd told Reese the truth.

"Yes. I thought it was fitting that she be named after her two grandmothers. Joy seemed appropriate, since Chrissy brought me so much happiness," she said.

He made a small sound of approval. "Mom would have liked that."

If the quick way he blinked his eyes was any indication, he liked it, too. And for some reason, that pleased Katie enormously.

"I just wish you had told me sooner," he finally said, his gaze burning into hers until she felt as though he could see deep inside her tattered heart.

Katie swallowed hard. "Quite frankly, I didn't plan to ever tell you. I figured you wouldn't want anything to do with us. But this year Chrissy started asking questions about her daddy. Why all of her friends had a father, but she didn't. Why her dad never visited or sent her birthday gifts. I thought perhaps I'd tell her the truth after she graduated from high school, when she was old enough to understand better. But then I saw you on the national news and I thought… I thought…" Her words trickled off on a sigh of frustration.

He finished the sentence for her. "You thought I might die and Chrissy wouldn't get the chance to know her father, is that it?"

She nodded, unwilling to tell a lie. "You work in a very dangerous profession."

He nodded. "Yes."

She wondered again if this was a mistake. Her deep, abiding faith in God had brought her to speak the truth.

One day, Chrissy would grow into a woman, and Katie didn't want her to be tormented by the unknown. Always wondering who her father was and what he was like. Katie had read once that kids who lost a parent when they were young frequently deified that parent. Thought their life would be better if only their lost mom or dad were around. It was natural for a kid to wonder about a missing parent. But this situation still wasn't easy for Katie.

"I almost can't believe this news. It's a bit much to take in," Reese said. Anger and cynicism filled his expressive eyes. He locked his jaw, hard as granite.

It served him right. She tried to forget all the hurt and resentment she felt toward this man, but she couldn't seem to let it go.

"You abandoned me. Remember?" She bit out the words, trying to contain her own anger.

"I never abandoned you," he said with incredulity. "We were kids. We never made any promises to each other. I didn't even know you were pregnant, Katie."

True. And she was just as guilty over what had happened between them. She could have told him no. She could have walked away and protected herself. But she hadn't. She'd loved him and given herself to him. Her most precious gift. She'd disappointed herself and her parents. But most of all, she'd disappointed the Lord. And now it was water under the bridge. She had to let it go and move on. But it hurt to know that Reese had never wanted her. Not then and not now.

"You deserted everyone in this town and you never looked back," she said. "You took off without caring who you might hurt. I think you made the mistake of thinking that no one in this town cared about you, and that wasn't true. You never came home to check on your mom. You didn't even return for your parents' funerals. And frankly, you have no right to be angry with me."

He raked a hand through his hair, showing his frustration. "Wait a minute, Katie. My father never called or wrote to tell me my mom had died. By the time I found out, she was already gone. I called three weeks after her funeral. I only spoke to my dad for a few minutes. He was drunk, as usual. A few months later, I received a package and a letter from Grace Chantry, telling me that my father had died, too."

Grace was a kind, elderly woman, one of the few people Katie had seen visiting Joy Hartnett, and likely Joy's only real friend. Katie didn't ask what was in the package Grace had sent to Reese. She told herself she didn't care. After Chrissy was born, she'd stopped asking Joy if she knew where Reese was. She was too afraid that her interest might draw questions about Chrissy's paternity. But right now, she was furious. She wanted him out of this truck. Wanted to dump him off at the cabin. To leave and never see him again.

The blood drained from his face and he sat very still. "You're right, though. I hurt my mom. I know that now. And I can't tell you how deeply I regret it. I wish I could have gotten my dad some help, but I was barely eighteen. I had no job or skills. No money. I didn't know how to help him, or how to get him into a rehabilitation program. And I didn't know that I'd hurt you, too. I never knew about Chrissy. That one night we had together, I...I thought it was just for fun. I had no idea we had created a child. I was young and thoughtless. I never considered the consequences of our actions, not even once. And all I can do now is ask for your forgiveness."

Whoa! She wasn't expecting this. Was his apology genuine? Katie narrowed her eyes, studying him, wondering if his look of contrition was real or fake. She didn't believe him. Except for her father, she didn't trust any man, especially Reese. She remembered the anxiety of finding herself pregnant, wondering what to do. Her panic had mingled with the joy of feeling her baby growing inside her, and then giving birth to Chrissy.

Alone.

Now something hardened inside Katie. Something cold and unforgiving. Reese had been the one to leave, not her. And she didn't love him anymore. Which was probably for the best. If he had stayed, she would have told him that she was pregnant. For the sake of their child, he might have asked her to marry him. And Katie was so in love with him back in those days that she would have done it. But it never would have worked. She didn't want to be trapped in a loveless marriage. Unwanted. A millstone around Reese's neck. They would have probably ended up divorced. And what kind of life would that have been for them and their child? They would have all been miserable.

"It's in the past now," she said.

"Not for me," he stated. "It's like it barely happened. I just found out that I'm a father. That I have a six-year-old daughter. I'm afraid it'll take a bit of time for me to adjust to the news."

Katie almost groaned out loud. She didn't want him to adjust to the idea, and yet she did. Right now, she didn't know what the future held for any of them. She didn't want trouble with this man, but now that seemed unavoidable.

"So, what do you want from me?" Reese asked.

"I don't want anything. Not one single thing," Katie said, sounding a bit outraged.

She sat in the driver's seat of her father's old truck and stared out the windshield. Reese got the impression she loathed him. His mind was buzzing. He couldn't believe this was happening. He'd come here to Minoa to recover from losing his hotshot crew, and now he'd gotten hit with this news. He couldn't absorb it fast enough.

"I'm finding all of this a bit difficult to swallow," he admitted.

She lifted her chin, looking proud and defiant. A wall stood between them. He'd felt it the moment she met him at the airport, but he hadn't understood it at the time. Now he knew. All those years ago, when he'd left town without telling her goodbye, he must have devastated her. And then, when she'd discovered she was pregnant, she must have been frantic, wondering what to do. How to handle the situation. Suddenly, her dreams of going to college and having a career had shriveled into nothing. Because of him. He'd let so many people down.

Reese took a deep breath, thinking about asking for a paternity test, just to make sure Chrissy was really his. But the dates lined up like clockwork. It hadn't been much, but he'd spent enough time with Chrissy to see the family resemblance. The familiarity he'd felt toward the child when they had first met finally made sense now. The clench of her jaw and the angle of her head were just like his father's. The curve of her mouth when she smiled reminded him of his mother. And every time he looked at her sweet face, he felt as though he were peering into his own eyes. The exact same shape and color as his. No wonder she looked so familiar to him. She was his. No doubt about it.

He turned to face Katie. Their gazes clashed, then locked. She glared right back, not looking friendly at all. Certainly not like a woman who loved him. And he didn't love her. There was no use pretending. Besides, he wasn't father material. And yet they had a child. It changed everything and nothing.

"So, when you found out I was returning to town, you decided it was time to tell me the truth?" he asked.

She nodded. "I just don't want you to hurt her."

Reese quirked his eyebrows. "You think I would do that?"

"I don't know. Would you?" Katie fired the question back, her voice thick with animosity.

He thought about all the years he'd missed of his child's life. He'd never seen Chrissy as a newborn baby. Never rocked her in his arms, fed her a bottle or heard her call him Daddy. And he had no one to blame but himself. Now, he didn't have a clue how to be a father to a six-year-old, but he realized he'd better learn fast. Because he'd been thrust into this situation whether he liked it or not.

"I have no intention of hurting anyone. I didn't come here to interrupt your lives," he said.

"Why did you come here?" she asked.

He hesitated, not wanting to tell her about visiting his mom's grave. It was a bit too personal. He wanted a quiet place to hide out until the news of what had happened died down and the media stopped hunting him. He just wanted to go home, but he didn't know where that was anymore.

"I came here to be alone," he said.

Katie's face stiffened and he realized he'd said the wrong thing.

"That suits me just fine. We can leave you alone. But I do have a couple of requests," she said.

"And what is that?" he asked.

"That you meet with Chrissy and spend a little time with her before you leave town again. I'd like all three of us to sit down together so you and I can explain to her that you're her father. I'd also like to have a picture of you two taken together. It doesn't have to be fancy. Just something that Chrissy can keep, to remember you by once you're gone. Can you do that without upsetting her?"

The hackles rose at the nape of his neck. Katie's words were insulting, but he didn't bite back. In dealing with his drunken father, he'd learned to hold his tongue and keep his thoughts to himself. Otherwise, he might find himself knocked across the room. Right now, Reese felt confused. He needed time to think about this. To plan and consider what he should do.

"Of course I can do that," he said.

She opened the door and got out. "Good. Now, let me show you the cabin. Then I better get home."

That was it? Somehow, he expected more. He had a child. Another person who was a part of him. His flesh and blood. He couldn't help feeling curious and intrigued, not fully understanding what it meant.

He got out of the vehicle. Shouldering his bag, he followed Katie up the rock path leading to the front door. The tall pine trees overhead swayed gently in the afternoon breeze. Looking about, he took in the litter of enormous pinecones and needles covering the front yard, along with several dead bushes. A huge fire hazard. Experienced as he was, Reese knew this property needed fifty feet of defensible space around it to ward off a forest fire. Maybe he could do something about that while he stayed here.

She unlocked the door and stepped inside. He was right behind her, blinking as his eyes adjusted to the dim interior. Katie opened the curtains at the windows, letting sunshine permeate the wide room.

A kitchen area with an old wood cookstove, a sink and cupboards sat in one corner, with a rustic table and chairs for eating meals. On the other side of the room, a simple rock fireplace filled one wall, with a sofa perched in front of it, along with two recliners and a coffee table nearby. An afghan and several throw pillows decorated the furnishings, along with battery-operated lamps sitting on the side tables. Pictures of mule deer hung on the walls. On one shelf, a pile of board games and books offered entertainment to anyone who was interested.

Reese's gaze swept over the cozy space and screeched to a halt when he saw several small framed pictures of Chrissy with her mom and grandparents. They were fishing together, laughing, having fun as a family. And once again he felt as though he didn't belong here. Yet something inside him wished that he could be a part of it all. But he wasn't. He'd fathered Chrissy and nothing more.

"There's no electricity or running water, so you'll have to rough it," Katie said. "There are plenty of gallon jugs of fresh water in the kitchen cupboards, for drinking and washing. The privy is out back. We've got extra batteries for the lights in the cabinet over there." She pointed at two battery-operated lanterns sitting on windowsills and jutted her chin toward a set of drawers.

Reese nodded, immune to the rural conditions. As a hotshot, he was well versed on roughing it. No big deal.

"This is more than I expected. Thank you," he said.

"There should be clean dishes and something to eat in here. There's wood out back for the cookstove." Katie walked into the kitchen area and rummaged around in the cupboards. She pulled out several cans and an opener and set them on the counter. Soup and some kind of vegetable.

"That will be fine," he said.

He was coasting on autopilot but felt as though he was lost in a fog. He still couldn't get past the news that he had a daughter, and he wondered how Katie could act so normal. And yet he detected the tension in her shoulders. She was angry with him.

"We'll bring you some more supplies tomorrow. Do you think you'll be okay until then?" she asked.

He nodded as he stepped over to the doorways leading to the two bedrooms. "Yes, I'll be fine."

He peered inside the first room, noticing the comfortable double bed with a handmade quilt, the pillows and the chest of drawers. Outside the window, he heard the ragged call of a blue jay. The peace and calm was exactly what he was after, and yet there was no peace in his heart.

"Remember, Mrs. Murdoch lives a quarter of a mile down the road, if you have an emergency," Katie said.

He nodded again, not knowing what else to say. He doubted Mrs. Murdoch would be too friendly. Not when she recalled that he and his friends had broken the taillights out of her husband's truck years earlier.

"Well, I better be going," Katie said, edging toward the open door. She glanced outside, as though desperate to flee.

"We'll talk some more tomorrow," he said, knowing he'd have more questions by then.

"Yeah, tomorrow," she agreed.

And then she was gone. He stood where he was, listening as she opened and slammed the door to her truck, then turned on the engine. The crackling of gravel beneath the tires told him that she was pulling out of the driveway. For one insane moment, he almost ran outside to call her back. To ask her to tell him more about Chrissy and her life here in town.

He resisted the urge. Right now, he needed time to think. To figure out what had happened to his life and if he wanted to fit into Chrissy's. Reese realized that he couldn't have a relationship with his daughter without going through Katie. The woman seemed to hate him, which bothered him for some odd reason. Normally, he didn't care what other people thought, especially not a girl from his past. But he did now. And looking around him, he'd never felt more alone in all his life.

Chapter Four

"There's Reese." Chrissy pointed out the window as Katie pulled into the driveway at the cabin the following morning.

The little girl clawed at the belt buckle on her booster seat before Katie could even shut off the truck engine.

"Chrissy, wait," she called.

The child didn't listen. She threw open the door and jumped down, then sprinted toward Reese. He stood in the yard, leaning against the long handle of a rake. With a glance, Katie took in his leather work gloves, faded blue jeans and the navy T-shirt that hugged every muscle of his chest and arms. Several tidy piles of pine needles, cones and dead bushes dotted the yard. Since yesterday afternoon, it appeared that he'd kept himself busy.

His gaze followed Chrissy as she raced toward him, crying his name. Then his eyes met Katie's, and her senses went on high alert. She watched his reactions like a mother hen, curious to see how he treated their daughter.

As she climbed out of the truck and headed over to join them, she heard Reese's greeting. "Hi, Chrissy. How are you?"

"I'm fine," the girl trilled in a happy voice.

Without being invited, she hugged Reese's long legs with open affection. Reese's face flooded with color, but Katie had to give him credit. He reached down and patted the child's shoulder in an awkward gesture that said he wasn't sure what else to do. And knowing how badly her daughter craved the attention of a father in her life, his actions brought tears to Katie's eyes.

"Look what I made at kindergarten." Chrissy held up a round, palm-sized object painted yellow, with a black grinning face.

Reese smiled and lines creased the corners of his eyes. Eyes that seemed so sad and guarded. "That's nice. What is it?"

"My pet rock," Chrissy said, as though it was obvious.

"Oh." Reese floundered, looking rather sheepish.

"I named it Emily. Teacher says whenever I'm feeling lonely, I can talk to Emily," she said. "But I know it isn't a real person. It's just a rock. And it's not as fun to talk to as Papa Charlie."

"I see." He nodded and his eyes sparkled, as though he was enchanted by the bubbly girl.

"I'd rather have a puppy or a kitten to talk to," Chrissy continued. "But Mommy says pets are a lot of work, they're expensive to feed and they make messes. Papa says he'll think about it, maybe for Christmas. He says it would be good to have a guard dog at the motel, but he's not sure he wants to potty train one. But that's what I really want."

"Yeah, um, dogs are nice. I had one when I was a kid." Reese blinked, looking slightly dazed by this conversation.

"You did? What was its name?"

"Duke," Reese responded.

"What happened to him?" Chrissy asked.

"He died when I was fourteen."

The girl's mouth quivered slightly. "Why?"

Reese gave a half laugh. "He got old, sweetheart."

Sweetheart.

Hearing Reese call her daughter that name did something to Katie. She felt territorial and possessive and didn't understand why.

"I wouldn't mind having a kitty with yellow and white stripes," Chrissy said.

"Yellow and white, huh? Well, maybe that's what you'll get for Christmas," he said.

"Okay, that's enough," Katie interjected gently. "You're gonna hug the stuffing out of Reese."

She didn't want Chrissy to overwhelm the guy. She tugged on her daughter's shoulders, pulling her back for a quick hug of her own.

Reese met Katie's eyes. For just a moment, she saw a bit of panic written across his face. As though he didn't know how to act. Then it was gone and she thought perhaps she'd imagined it. Katie couldn't help feeling some compassion for him. But just a little.

The sound of an engine coming into the yard caused Katie to turn. Her dad parked his blue truck behind her vehicle and climbed out with his cane. In addition to these two trucks, Katie and her father owned a car, which she usually drove around town to get to work at her job at the newspaper office and to run errands.

"Hi, Reese. Did you have a good night?" Charlie called.

"I did, thank you. It's real quiet up here." Reese gave a half-hearted wave.

"Yeah, I sleep like a rock when we stay up here. It looks like you've been doing some yard work." Charlie jutted his chin toward the tidy piles of debris that Reese had raked up.

He shrugged. "It's the least I can do to repay you for letting me stay here. It's good to clear the area around your property, in case there's a wildfire."

"That's kind of you. I've been meaning to get up here and take care of it, but the motel keeps me pretty busy. Seems like there's always a clogged toilet or other repair needing to be done. Right now, I'm getting ready to fix the roof on the shed. If we get a rainstorm, it'll soak everything inside." Charlie chuckled.

"Dad, I told you I don't want you climbing up on that roof," Katie objected. "You just had hip replacement surgery four months ago."

"Maybe I can help you with that," Reese said.

"No need. I can do it," Charlie said.

"Dad..." Katie began. But she wasn't sure what to say. She didn't want her father up on ladders, but neither did she want Reese hanging around the motel more than necessary.

"It'd be my pleasure. Staying busy helps take my mind off things." Reese didn't elaborate on what those things were, but Katie knew.

Hmm. She didn't remember Reese ever helping out when he was young. Cleaning up the yard here had been a chore that kept nagging at her. It was kind of Reese to take care of it for them, but that didn't mean she'd forgiven him.

"Are you settled in?" Charlie asked.

"Yeah. It's beautiful here. Last night was the first time I've slept through since..." His words trailed off, his eyes suddenly filled with a sad, vacant look.

Katie knew what he'd been about to say. He hadn't slept through the night since he'd lost his crew. She wondered if nightmares haunted him. She'd heard stories about men and women going into combat and returning with post-traumatic stress disorder. From what she knew, fighting walls of flames could be just like going to war. The adrenaline. The fear. She hoped Reese wasn't suffering from PTSD but then reminded herself that it wasn't her business. She shouldn't care.

But she did.

"What's with the two vehicles?" Reese gestured toward the driveway.

Charlie reached into the back of his truck and hefted a cardboard box. "I have two trucks. You can borrow my old wood truck while you're staying here. It isn't much. I only use it to go up into the mountains and cut firewood for our stove at the motel. Tossing chunks of wood into the back causes a lot of scratches and dents and I don't want to mar my newer vehicle. The wood truck isn't pretty, but it runs well."

"Oh." Reese frowned in confusion. "You didn't need to do that. I can get around well enough. I'm in pretty good shape and enjoy walking."

"Nonsense. You can't walk all the way into town. It'd take you hours. We don't want you stuck out here all alone, especially if some reporters show up. Katie and Chrissy will ride back home with me when we leave. You'll use the wood truck as long as you're here." It wasn't a question, and there was a note of finality in Charlie's voice.

"Okay, thanks. Can I help you with that?" Reese reached for the box, but Charlie waved him off.

"Nah, I got it. We brought you some food supplies, too." Using his cane, he limped toward the cabin, carrying the box beneath his free arm.

Reese swallowed. "Thank you, but you didn't need to bring me food, either."

"Of course we did. You're our guest. And a man's got to eat. But be sure you seal up your garbage. We've got bears in these mountains and they like to root around in the trash." Charlie's deep voice sounded cheerful.

Katie tossed her father a withering glare, but he took no notice. She thought he was trying too hard. As a loving father, he wanted her to be happy. But right now, she didn't like that he was being so nice to Reese.

"I picked out the cocoa flakes and apples for you. They're my favorites," Chrissy said, her button nose crinkling.

"They are, huh?" Reese reached out and rubbed the top of her head. She beamed up at him in return.

Inwardly, Katie trembled. Watching this man interact with her child made her nervous. Other than Charlie, she wasn't used to having a father figure in Chrissy's life. She felt hopeful and jealous at the same time. Ready to whisk her child away at a moment's notice. She couldn't understand why the girl had latched on to Reese so easily. Chrissy was normally shy around strangers.

"I appreciate all you've done for me," Reese said.

"It's our pleasure…isn't it, Katie?" Charlie said.

She frowned. She didn't want her father to expect too much, but she couldn't say that right now. Not in front of Reese and Chrissy. "Um, yeah."

Clasping the box, Charlie nudged Chrissy with his elbow. "Hey, bug. Why don't you come and help me put these groceries away in the cabin? Then we can make some lunch."

"Sure!" The girl skipped ahead of him.

Reese's gaze followed the child, as though he couldn't believe what he was seeing. A hint of tenderness filled his eyes and Katie wasn't surprised. Chrissy was sweet and guileless. A person would have to be hard-hearted not to find her completely adorable.

And suddenly Katie found herself all alone with the man she could neither reject nor accept.

"Have you…?" she began.

"Do you…?" Reese said at the same time.

They stopped and gazed at one another for a moment. Then they laughed.

"I'm sorry. You go first," Katie said.

Reese held up a hand. "No, ladies first."

Once again she was surprised by his good manners. "I was just wondering if you've had a chance to think about what I told you yesterday."

He inclined his head. "Yes, I've thought about little else."

"And?" she pressed.

He released a slow sigh. "It's been a lot to take in."

"Yes, I'm sure it is. But what do you want to do?"

He pulled off his leather gloves and shoved them into his pants pocket. "I'm not sure what you expect."

She bristled. He'd always bailed out on his responsibilities. Why had she dared to hope he might want to be some kind of father to her child?

"You could take Chrissy for an ice cream cone at the drive-in, or take her to the park for a playdate," she said.

He hesitated. "I've never spent any time with little kids. I don't know how to act around them."

"Chrissy's pretty talkative, so she'll probably provide most of the conversation. Why don't you just try being yourself?" she suggested.

"I can do that. But what if she cries? Could I spend some time with her over at your place, to get to know her better first?"

"Of course, if that makes you feel more comfortable. But Chrissy isn't much of a crier." Katie thought visits at her home would be perfect. She had no problem with Reese being around Chrissy, as long as she or Charlie was present. She still didn't know this man well enough to let him take off alone with her daughter.

"What does she like to do?" he asked, fidgeting with his rake.

The thought that he might need a little guidance amused Katie.

"She likes to watch kid movies, color with crayons and play with her dolls. How about if you come over to the motel for some short visits? That way, you can get to know her. And maybe you could have dinner with us tomorrow night."

There. That was good. Dinner would provide the opportunity for Reese and Chrissy to be together, but still allow Katie to keep an eye on them. Charlie would be there, too, to help alleviate any possible tension between them. It was a start.

"That sounds good. I'll come over tomorrow."

"Fine, but keep in mind that I'm not always home. You should call first, to make sure Chrissy's there. I'm coordinating some service projects for our church congregation. When Chrissy's not in school, she tags along with me."

He released a sigh of relief. "If I find her home, I'll spend time with her. But it sounds like Charlie could use some help with his roofing project, too."

"Yes, Dad won't admit it, but he's getting older. I'm afraid of him taking a bad tumble. I'm sure he could use your help, if you can spare the time. The shed's in the back, so you'd be hidden if any reporters show up. Tomorrow I'll be working at the front desk most of the day, but we'd appreciate it."

"Then I'll come over in the morning. And thanks."

Thanks. He was saying that a lot lately. Maybe Charlie was right. Maybe Reese had changed.

"How about some lunch?" Charlie called from the cabin. "Chrissy and I made sandwiches for all of us."

"That sounds great," Reese called back.

In gentlemanly fashion, he waited for Katie to precede him up the path. Knowing he was behind her, she felt self-conscious, and her spine tingled. Forcing herself to walk in a steady stride, she told herself everything was going well. She'd finally told Reese that he was the father of her child. He'd accepted the news without causing a big scene, and he even wanted to get to know Chrissy better. And then what?

Katie had no idea what the future held. There were a zillion questions milling around inside her brain. Where had Reese been all these years? She assumed he wasn't married or the national news would have mentioned his family. There would be time to ask him these questions later on. Since she'd graduated from high school, she'd learned to take things one day at a time. But now that Reese was back in her life, she figured she had better switch to taking things moment by moment.

Reese followed Katie into the cabin. Charlie was setting paper plates filled with sandwiches on the table. The air smelled sweet, like chocolate. Reese saw the cause. A plastic package of brownies sat open on the counter.

A noise came from the living area and Reese glanced to his left. Chrissy was crouched next to the wall, rifling through his duffel bag.

Katie gasped. "Christine Joy Ashmore! That doesn't belong to you. Get out of it."

She hurried over to her daughter, her face flushed with

embarrassment. The little girl jerked around and dropped Reese's shaving kit. It hit the wood floor with a thump.

Christine Joy Ashmore.

Reese couldn't help noticing that Katie had given the girl her own last name. Not his. He shouldn't be surprised. No one knew he was her father. But hearing Chrissy called by another surname caused something possessive to rise up inside Reese. Something he didn't understand.

He looked at Katie. Really looked at her for the first time. All he saw was a beautiful, confident woman who was trying to do what was best for her child. And in that moment, he felt that familiar twinge of guilt that he hadn't been here for her when she really needed him. But he also felt an edge of panic. He'd come here to be left alone. Then he planned to leave again. He had never wanted to be tied down. Not to an old high school friend and her cute little daughter.

Correction. *Their* daughter. He had to get used to that. He now had people depending on him. A responsibility to look after this little girl and her mother.

No, Katie didn't need his help. She'd proved that she was capable on her own. He could leave anytime he wanted to, couldn't he? Of course he could. Katie would take care of Chrissy. It wasn't as if they were homeless and didn't know where their next meal would come from. They were okay without him. So why did he get a sinking feeling in the pit of his stomach whenever he thought of never seeing them again?

"I was just looking for something in Reese's duffel bag," Chrissy said.

The child stared at the floor, appearing rather dismal. Something softened inside Reese's heart. He reminded himself that whether they knew each other or not, this wasn't a stranger anymore. This was his daughter. His. And some hidden instinct caused him to walk over to the girl.

He bent to pick up things of his that Chrissy had strewn across the floor. A couple novels he'd been reading. Several pairs of clean socks and shirts, which had previously been folded in tidy piles. He didn't know kids could be such a nuisance, but he wasn't really bothered by Chrissy's curiosity. He glanced at her bouncing, reddish-blond ponytail and guileless smile. It was difficult to be irritated by such a cute little girl.

His little girl.

"What were you looking for? Maybe I can help you find it." Down on his haunches, he spoke in a gentle voice, highly conscious of Katie watching him closely from nearby.

His offer won an instant smile from Chrissy and she met his eyes. "I was looking for a compass. You're a firefighter, so I know you must have one. Teacher said you can always find your true north with a compass." Then her forehead furrowed in consternation. "What's a true north?"

He reached into the duffel, rummaged around until he found what she was after, then held up a small leather case. He opened it as he spoke. "When you're lost, your true north is how you find your way."

He pulled out his compass, which he rested on his open palm. The shiny black needle slid smoothly into the northern position. Katie leaned over to see, too, and he caught her scent. Something delicate and tangy. Like citrus.

"See the arrow?" he asked, pointing at the device.

Chrissy nodded in awe, her eyes wide. "Yes."

"Right now, it's pointing due north. That's what the *N*

stands for. No matter where you are, it will always point north." He handed the compass to the girl and she held it reverently with both hands.

"So, is that the direction I should go if I'm ever lost?" she asked.

He chuckled, amazed at her curiosity and intellect. Knowing she was his child, he felt a mixture of wonder and pride. "That depends. If you know that your destination is in the east, then you should head that way. But before you can find east, you have to know where true north is. Understand?"

He doubted that she did. The concept was pretty complicated for one so young.

"Ah." Chrissy nodded. "So if I know which way is north, then I can figure out which way is east. Then I'll know which way to go."

Wow! He didn't know any other six-year-olds, but he figured Chrissy's acumen was exceptional. She'd grasped the concept of orienteering without a lot of explanation.

"That's right," he said, delighted by her achievement.

"Maybe we'll have to get you your own compass," Charlie suggested from the kitchen area.

"Yeah, then I can find my true north anytime I'm lost," Chrissy said.

That gave Reese an idea. He thought of all the birthdays and Christmas gifts he'd missed with Chrissy. All the quiet moments when he might have taught her about things like orienteering. Maybe while he was in town, he could make up for lost time.

Chrissy smiled, her green eyes sparkling, and he felt enthralled. He hadn't known about her, but Katie had given him a beautiful and amazing child. He didn't deserve anything this wonderful, but he was beyond grateful. Because at this difficult time in his life, Chrissy was like a soothing salve to his tattered heart.

"Let's eat before the sandwiches dry out," Charlie urged.

Chrissy handed the compass back to Reese, sliding it carefully into his hands. She seemed to know that the instrument was expensive and should be handled with care.

As they walked to the table, pulled out the wooden chairs and sat in them, Reese stole surreptitious looks at Katie. Both she and Chrissy folded their arms and bowed their heads while Charlie said a quick blessing on their meal. Then Katie placed apple slices on Chrissy's plate.

"May I have a brownie, please?" the girl asked politely, turning to look at the counter.

"After you've eaten your sandwich and fruit." Katie tapped her daughter's plate.

Chrissy frowned. "Aw, do I have to?"

"Yes, bug." Charlie laughed.

"Okay." She smiled good-naturedly, swinging her legs back and forth as she picked up her ham-and-cheese sandwich and bit into the soft bread.

Katie reached over and brushed a long strand of hair back from the child's cheek. In Katie's eyes, Reese saw the blatant love and adoration of a mother. Watching them together, he couldn't help thinking Katie was a good mom. But that didn't mean they would ever be together. It was obvious that Katie disliked him. Now they had to do the best they could for Chrissy.

He bit into his own sandwich, feeling strangely calm with the happy chatter around him. He could almost forget the tragedy that had brought him here in the first place. He'd come home to be alone but now found himself surrounded by this family.

But Reese couldn't stay. Sooner or later, he'd have to leave again.

Chapter Five

"I told you, Reese isn't interested in giving anyone his story." Katie gazed steadily at Tom Klarch, her editor from the *Minoa Daily News*.

He stood in the office at the motel, resting his forearms against the counter as he leaned toward her. It was late morning and she'd called to tell him she wouldn't be into work today. She'd been stunned when he'd shown up here.

His beady eyes scoured her face, as though searching for the truth. "You went to school with him, Katie. He'll talk to you."

She doubted it. Reese had made his feelings on the topic clear. "It's been a long time since high school. I barely know him now. He's not interested in chatting about his hotshot crew."

"A smart girl like you ought to be able to get him to tell you what happened," Tom said.

She looked away, wishing he hadn't arrived unexpectedly. She'd been working the reception counter and felt cornered. "I would never write his story without his permission," she said.

"Then get his permission," he insisted.

She glanced toward the open window. Sunlight

streamed through the room, and a gentle breeze filtered through the screen door leading out to the parking lot. Katie released a quiet sigh, wishing she could slip outside and go for a long walk by herself. She'd been trying to think things through but so far hadn't found any answers. Thankfully, Chrissy was at morning kindergarten. Charlie had gone to the hardware store, then would stop and pick her up on his way home.

"If you don't want to write the story, I will. But I need the details," the editor said.

"It's not that, Tom. I'd love to write his story. But the guy is hurting."

"So build some trust with him. Use your pretty face, if you have to, but get him to confide in you."

She almost laughed. Her pretty face? Reese had never found her attractive. At least, not in high school. The only man to tell her she was pretty was her father, and that didn't count. If the media discovered that Chrissy was Reese's daughter, they'd park on her doorstep, hounding her for information and slathering embarrassing articles across the front page of every newspaper. Katie didn't want to subject Chrissy to such a circus. Now that she'd told Reese the truth, she feared the news might spread. When she saw him again, she'd make a point of asking him not to tell anyone, at least not until the reporters left town.

"I won't build a relationship with Reese just so I can get a story out of him," she insisted.

"Why not?" Tom asked.

If he only knew.

She held out one hand. "Because it's dishonest and sleazy. I can write the story, but I won't let it be published unless Reese agrees."

"If you wrote his story, we could get an exclusive that

might get picked up nationally. It could mean big things for you and me. Maybe get both of us out of this little town," Tom said.

Katie frowned. For years, she thought she would love to leave Minoa and go somewhere else, to build a real career in a big city. Now she loved Minoa. And what about Dad? He'd be all alone if she took Chrissy and left.

She stood up from the chair at the computer. Rounding the counter, she hoped to show Tom the door. Lifting her chin, she met his steady gaze. "Reese came to Minoa to escape the media. He's not here, Tom. Can't you leave him alone, at least until he's not hurting so much?"

She didn't know why she was defending Reese. Just like when the news reporters had clogged their parking lot, she felt protective of him. She told herself it was because she feared people might find out he was Chrissy's father.

"That's good! He's hurting. You can really play on that emotion," Tom said.

"Not without his permission," she stated again.

At that precise moment, the subject of their conversation walked into the room. Reese stood there, a slight frown crinkling his handsome face, his wide shoulders filling the doorway. Katie hoped he hadn't overheard her conversation with Tom.

The screen door clapped shut behind him. Katie stared with an open mouth and shifted her weight. He was early. She didn't expect him until later.

In one hand, he held a small package wrapped in bright yellow paper that was decorated with pink bunny rabbits. An overly large white bow was perched on top. In his other hand, he held a bouquet of white daisies. The green tissue paper around the long stems crackled. While she tried to tell herself that she didn't really care what

Reese thought, she couldn't help sympathizing with him for not wanting to talk about the fire. It irritated her that Tom wouldn't take no for an answer.

"Hi, there," Reese said, the corners of his mouth lifting in an uncertain half smile. A smile that still had the power to turn her insides to mush. But that wasn't going to sway her. He was Chrissy's father, nothing more.

"Hello," Katie said, wishing Reese hadn't shown up just then. Not holding flowers and a gift, and not with Tom standing there gawking like a buzzard ready to swoop in for the kill.

The editor's gaze centered on the bouquet and he tossed a knowing look in Katie's direction. A slow, conniving smile curved his thick lips. No doubt he thought Reese was interested in her and she could wheedle a story out of him. But Katie couldn't. She didn't want to get close enough to Reese for him to reveal his feelings to her. Nor did she want the media hounding her because they thought she and Reese were close. She also didn't want Tom to think she'd just lied to him about Reese's whereabouts. Why couldn't people leave them alone? And why did she even care?

An uncomfortable silence filled the room and Reese glanced from her to Tom. "Am I interrupting something?" he asked, his forehead creased with doubt.

"No, of course not," Katie said, a bit too quickly.

"You're Reese Hartnett, aren't you?" Thrusting out his hand, Tom brushed her aside.

A glimmer of distrust crossed Reese's face as he tentatively shook hands with the man. "Who are you?"

"Tom Klarch. I own the *Minoa Daily News*. Katie's my star reporter." His boisterous voice filled the office.

Reese glanced at Katie, his eyes wary. She almost laughed at being called a star reporter. For two years, she'd been submitting a variety of exciting articles for Tom to publish. Topics included governmental budget oversight, a terror threat in Reno, drugs and violence in the local high school. Time after time, Tom rejected every story and told her she was still too inexperienced. He'd assigned her to the obituaries and recipe column instead. Mundane issues she couldn't care less about. Then articles similar to the ones she had submitted would soon appear in the paper. A word or two had been changed, but it was obvious that Tom had stolen her entire story. Because she wanted to keep her job, she hadn't objected to the plagiarism. But she had almost given up hope of ever seeing her work taken seriously.

Reese's spine stiffened and he drew back ever so slightly, his eyes filled with suspicion. She hated for him to think that she had invited Tom here. That he might believe she'd conspired with the editor to get Reese's story.

"I'd like to interview you," Tom continued.

Reese was shaking his head even before Tom finished his sentence. "Sorry, I'm not interested."

"How about if we talk off the record?" Tom pressed.

A deep scowl creased Reese's forehead and his eyes narrowed. "I have nothing to say to you off the record, on the record or anything in between."

Tom laughed. "Surely you know the press is going to write about you no matter what. You're the man that survived. It's big news. People care that your entire crew died. This is your chance to tell your side. You can help me get it down right."

Reese's jaw hardened as anger flashed in his eyes. "I said no."

"You sure? I'd be willing to pay you. I'm certain we could come to some lucrative agreement. I'd make it worth your while." Tom's voice sounded coaxing and pushy.

Backing toward the door, Reese shook his head. He looked desperate to flee. To be anywhere but here.

The editor reached into his pocket and pulled out a business card. When Reese didn't take it, Tom slid it into the front pocket of Reese's short-sleeved shirt. "If you change your mind, give me a call. Or talk to Katie. She could write a fair story for you."

Again, Reese didn't reply. He just stood there, his eyes chips of ice, his face hard as granite.

Finally, Tom took the hint. "Well, I better get back to the office. Think about it." He tossed an expectant look at Katie. "I'll see you tomorrow."

She nodded, dreading it. No job was worth the price of her integrity. She bit her tongue to keep from saying what she really thought. More than once, Tom's aggressive behavior had been a big turnoff for her. She'd put up with his badgering for two years because she wanted a career outside her work at the motel. In this small town, her job choices were seriously limited. But more and more, Tom's shady manners were getting on her nerves.

With a greasy smile, he slid past Reese and stepped outside. The moment the door closed behind him, Katie breathed with relief.

"I'm sorry about that. He just showed up, asking where you were," she explained.

Reese hiked one eyebrow, his gaze resting on her face. "Did you tell him I was staying at your cabin on Cove Mountain?"

"Of course not," she assured him. "Nor did I agree to publish a story about you. At least, not without your permission."

He inclined his head, but his eyes held a hint of doubt. "I appreciate that."

"I don't want trouble, Reese," she said. "I think for now, it's important that people don't know you're Chrissy's father. At least until the media frenzy settles down."

"I agree. Chrissy is innocent in all of this and I don't want her to get hurt," he said.

Whew! Katie was glad he understood and agreed with her motivation.

"Did anyone see you pull into the back of the motel?" she asked.

"No, I was careful. I did a little shopping in town, but I wore a baseball cap and kept my head down to hide my face. When I came here, I took the long way around, to ensure I wasn't followed." He tugged on the brim of his cap for emphasis. "I parked in your garage. I hope that's okay."

"Yes. I doubt Tom will tell anyone you're here. He's too anxious to get your story for himself. He won't want to share." She glanced at the flowers. "You look like you're going to a birthday party."

"I am, sort of." He stepped forward and held out the bouquet. "These are for you."

She backed up. Confusion filled her mind. He was giving her flowers? What on earth for?

"Don't worry," he said. "They're just to say thank you…for Chrissy. I wasn't here when she was born, so I never got to thank you for giving me a daughter. I thought I should tell you now."

She stood there, frozen in place. Someone could have knocked her over with a piece of string. His words sounded genuine. Something she'd never expected. In all these years, no one except her dad had given her flowers. Reese was her first love, her first kiss, her first everything. But no more. If he thought a bouquet of daisies could make up for lost time, he was dead wrong.

"I'm afraid I can't accept them," she said.

"Why not?"

Because she'd loved him once, that's why. And because she didn't trust him. She didn't want him to be the first man to give her flowers. Not when it didn't mean anything.

"Because…because I just can't," she murmured.

"Sure you can. They're just flowers, Katie. Between friends," he said.

Friends? Well, okay. Maybe she could do friends. After all, they did have a child together.

"All right. Friends. Thank you." She reached out and took the flowers, her heart filled with misgivings. His fingers brushed hers and she drew back quickly, feeling the warmth zinging up her arm like an electric current.

He didn't seem to notice as he held up the wrapped gift. "And this is for Chrissy. A belated birthday present."

Katie stared in dumb shock. She'd wanted Reese to be involved in Chrissy's life, but she hadn't thought it through. Hadn't considered what it might mean to her and her daughter.

"It's Easter wrap," she said, focusing on the little rabbits.

He glanced down, his face flushing red. "I'm sorry. It's all Grover's Grocery had at the moment. It was this or wedding wrap. They'll be getting some birthday wrap in next week on their delivery truck, but I didn't want to wait."

Katie hid a smile of amusement, wondering about the contents. It was way too small for a dolly or some other little-girl toy. So what could it be?

"I'm sure Chrissy will love the bunnies," she said.

"Is she here?" he asked, craning his head to see into the back office.

"No, she's still at kindergarten. Dad left a while ago to run some errands before he picks her up. She should be here in time for lunch."

"Maybe I can make myself useful in the meantime. I'm here to work on the new roof for your shed."

"We can hire a man from town to take care of that," she said, wishing he'd leave, yet hoping he'd stay. Oh, she didn't know what she wanted anymore. Her mind whirled in confusion. For Chrissy's sake, she tried to be polite.

"I'd like to help out," he said. "And quite frankly, I'm bored and would like to repay you and Charlie for your kindness. Besides, repairing a roof is right up my alley. I'm good at that kind of work."

Again, she detected a note of sincerity in him. But being near this man befuddled her.

"Payment isn't necessary. We're glad we could help," she said.

"I understand. But do you mind if I head out back to take a look at the roof anyway?" he asked.

"Go ahead. You'll find tools and supplies inside the shed."

What else could she say? He couldn't get to know Chrissy if he wasn't around here. Katie would just have to get used to him. For the time being.

He flashed a charming grin, turned and headed out back, as though happy to have something to do. He whistled as he went, a lilting tune she'd never heard before. His stride was quick, a confident swagger that said he had a purpose. And she realized that she hadn't seen him this happy since he'd arrived in town.

Watching him go, she wondered how she could ever get through the rest of the day with him hanging around.

She'd invited him to dinner, but now she thought it was a mistake. He'd probably be here for lunch, too. Sooner or later, they'd have to tell Chrissy that Reese was her father. It was inevitable that the girl would become attached to the man…just in time for him to leave town again and break Chrissy's heart.

Reese slid the shingle rake beneath several old roof tiles and pried them up. After dropping the rotted slates into a trash bin on the ground below, he repeated the action in another section, moving in an orderly manner. He'd retrieved a ladder from inside the shed, then climbed up on the roof, and had been working for twenty minutes. Even with the hot sun beating down on him, it felt good to be doing something useful. In fact, he remembered a time when he'd helped his father do this chore. One of the rare times when his dad wasn't drunk and angry at the world. A good memory Reese wanted to hold on to.

The exposed tar paper showed corrosion where it needed to be replaced. No problem. Charlie had a couple rolls of roofing felt sitting next to the riding lawn mower inside. In fact, Reese had noticed strips of metal drip edge, as well as boxes of new shingles and one-inch roofing nails. Everything he needed to complete the project. He figured he'd have the work finished by the end of the day.

"Ouch!" Reese dropped the shingle rake. He hadn't been paying attention and had pinched his thumb. Pulling off his leather gloves, he shook his hand to ease the sting.

"Reese?"

He turned and looked down. Katie stood below, her head tilted up as she watched him. A tall, muscular man with dark, curly hair and steely blue eyes stood beside her. Reese tensed, thinking this must be another news reporter.

"Yes?" Reese sounded a bit too defensive. He couldn't help feeling suspicious of everyone he met.

Katie made the introductions. "This is Sean Nash. He's the superintendent of the Minoa Hotshot Crew. Their base is here in town. I thought you might like to meet him."

Oh. Another wildfire fighter. But that didn't matter. Reese didn't want to talk to any colleagues, either.

Sean lifted an arm to shield his eyes against the glare of the sun. "I'm glad to meet you. It looks like you're staying busy."

Reese heard no censure in the man's voice, but he stiffened just the same. Right now, his crew should still be alive and he should be in Colorado, fighting wildfires with them. Not here in Minoa, shingling the roof of Charlie's shed.

"Yeah, it's good to stay busy," he said.

In a glance, Reese took in Sean's spruce-green pants and navy T-shirt with his hotshot logo imprinted on the left front side in white lettering. Reese had worn a similar uniform when he was on the job. He wanted to feel comfortable with this man. After all, he was a comrade… someone who understood how close a hotshot crew became. Like family. But then Reese thought better of it. As the leader of the Minoa Hotshots, Sean was undoubtedly experienced enough to make his own judgments about what had happened to Reese's team. And right now, Reese didn't want to hear any more criticism.

"Can you come down here?" Katie asked.

Reese didn't want to, but something in her gentle voice caused him to obey. For some reason, he hated the thought of disappointing her. He shimmied down the ladder and stood next to her. When he spoke to Sean, he tried not to sound too gruff. "What do you want?"

Sean slid his hands into his pants pockets, a congenial smile on his face. "I'd like to offer you a job."

Reese frowned, thinking he'd heard wrong. "A job?"

"Yeah. On my hotshot crew. I know you no longer have a team of your own, and I have an opening for a second assistant superintendent."

"A second?" Reese asked.

"Yeah, Rollo Simpson is my first assistant, but he's out on FMLA right now. His wife and one of his daughters were recently killed in a car accident."

Reese inwardly cringed. His troubles paled in comparison. Even so, he didn't think he wanted to fight fires anymore.

"I'm really hurting for leadership," Sean continued. "It'd be a permanent, year-round position with full benefits. If you're interested, we could use someone with your experience and skills."

An assistant superintendent. All the other positions on a hotshot crew were seasonal jobs. A month earlier, Reese would have jumped at such an opportunity. He'd worked hard as a crew boss, hoping one day he'd get a promotion like this. A dream come true.

But not anymore.

Reese glanced at Katie. She stood quietly listening, her face neutral. He couldn't even contemplate accepting such a job. The memory of losing his team was still too strong. The cloying smoke. The broiling flames. The screams of pain. The thought of fighting wildfires again terrified him. He couldn't be an assistant superintendent in charge of other people's lives. No way, no how.

"How…how did you know I was in town? How do you know I'm a good firefighter?" Reese asked.

Sean shrugged. "Your forest supervisor called me. He gave you an outstanding reference. We both think you're the right man for this job."

"Ah." Reese nodded. He'd told his supervisor where he was staying. The investigation into the deaths of his crew was ongoing and they might need to speak with him again.

"With his recommendation, I feel completely comfortable offering you this job," Sean said.

Reese swallowed hard. "Did he… Did he tell you what happened?"

Katie shifted her weight, standing a bit closer to him. At first he thought it was a protective gesture, to silently offer her support. But that couldn't be right. He'd seen the distrust in her eyes when he'd given her the flowers. And when she'd told him about Chrissy, she'd seemed wary and nervous. Like she didn't really want him here but had no choice. And then her newspaper editor had shown up at the motel. Reese hoped she wasn't angling for a story like the other reporters he'd encountered. Surely she wouldn't do that to him. Would she?

Sean lifted his head and met Reese's eyes. "Yes, I know what happened. But I also know it wasn't your fault. Your fire management officer said that you're a highly qualified firefighter and he wished you had been the lookout at the time. If so, your team might still be alive."

Ah, that hurt. Because Reese had found out later that the investigation team believed Logan, one of his buddies assigned as their lookout that day, had fallen asleep on the job. Reese had been on his way up the mountain to relieve Logan when the burnover had occurred. Reese had stood on the promontory and watched helplessly as his entire crew had died. But hearing Logan disparaged in any way made Reese feel defensive and angry. No matter their failings, Reese felt loyal to every man on his team. After all, they'd been working on that wildfire for several days with no sleep. They were beyond exhausted, but the command station hadn't let them rest. Instead, they'd pushed the crew beyond their endurance and it had cost them dearly.

Thinking about it now made Reese tremble. His heart beat like a hydraulic drill and his breath came heavy to his lungs. A wave of panic washed over him, but he fought it off. Post-traumatic stress disorder, his doctor called it. But Reese couldn't fall apart now. Not here in front of Katie.

"Reese, are you all right?" she asked, lifting a hand and resting it on his arm.

His face must have given his feelings away. Her touch brought him back to reality, but he didn't want her pity. He didn't want anything from her. He nodded, trying to swallow against the hard lump lodged in his throat.

She dropped her hand but stayed close beside him. For some reason, her presence gave him the composure he needed to hold it together.

"I'm…I'm not sure I want to fight wildfires anymore. I don't know what I want to do now," he said in all honesty.

Sean exhaled a deep sigh, then spoke in a gentle voice. "I feared as much. Believe me, I understand how you feel."

Yeah, sure he did. No one knew how he felt.

"I lost my best friend while fighting fires two summers ago," Sean continued. "I was the squad leader in charge, so I blamed myself for what happened. Zach Carpenter and I were trapped in a chimney area. I never should have taken him there to work, but we thought we could get a jump on the blaze. At the time, Zach's sister was a member of my crew and we were engaged to be married. But losing Zach caused a horrible rift that broke us apart. I almost died with Zach, and losing him made me question everything I used to believe in. My profession, my relationship with my fiancée, my faith in God. I was pretty lost for a long time."

Hmm. Maybe Sean did understand what he was going through.

"What helped you find your way?" Reese asked quietly. He'd give almost anything if he could figure this out and find the peace he hungered for.

Sean shrugged. "Tessa refused to give up on me. Don't get me wrong. She was angry at first. She believed I must have done something to get her brother killed. It took both of us a long time to realize it was no one's fault. It just happened. But she encouraged me to rely on the Lord. To hand my grief and fears over to Him. It wasn't easy, but finally, I did. And it made all the difference in the world. I'm not saying that all my problems are over. There are days when I think about losing Zach and it's still like a knife in my heart. But my faith in God has allowed me to cope with what happened. To know that the Lord loves each one of us and has our lives in His control. Tessa and I were married last December. We'll never forget Zach, but we've learned how to get past the grief."

"Congratulations," Reese said, unable to muster much enthusiasm. His sorrow still felt like heavy chains resting across his shoulders. He couldn't seem to get free of it no matter what he did.

Reese wanted to be friends with this man but wasn't sure he dared. Between his childhood, growing up with an alcoholic father and the events of the past couple of weeks, he had become distrustful of people. It seemed they all wanted to use him for their own ends. He was happy that Sean had found peace, but it still left Reese nowhere. It all sounded nice, but he didn't think he could turn to God for help with his heartache. He'd never been a praying man. Not as a teenager growing up in his father's home, and not now that he was an adult. He'd learned to rely on no one but himself. And that was enough. Or at least, it used to be. Now he wasn't so sure.

Sean reached into his pocket, pulled out a business card and handed it to Reese. "You'll need some time to recover from what happened. I can hold this job open for a little while longer, until you're ready. And when that time comes, the Minoa Hotshots are here to help. Anytime you need to talk, I'm available to listen."

Reese took the card, trying not to crumple it in his fist. Instead, he forced himself to be polite. After all, what had happened wasn't Sean's fault and he was only trying to help. "Thanks. I appreciate it. Really, I do."

And he meant it. Sean might be the only person he knew who really did understand what he was going through.

"Well, I better get back to work. I'll see you around." Sean nodded, then turned and walked away.

"Are you really okay?" Katie asked when they were alone.

Reese couldn't look at her. He just nodded, feeling empty inside. Already, he'd shown this woman too much weakness. He knew she harbored resentment toward him. He didn't want to make it any worse by telling her about his guilt and post-traumatic stress disorder.

"You really don't think you'll return to firefighting?" she asked.

He bowed his head and stared at the steel tips of his work boots. "I don't know. My entire team is gone and I'm not sure I want to work with a strange crew."

But the truth was he didn't know if he could face the fire again. Not without panicking. Not without being overcome by the harsh memories. And he didn't want to endanger anyone else's life because he couldn't do his job to the best of his abilities.

"Then what will you do to earn a living?" she asked.

He shrugged. "I'm not sure yet. I've thought that maybe I'd move to Reno and see if I can find some work there."

"Doing what?" she asked.

"Maybe construction. I'm pretty good with my hands and I'm a hard worker."

Reno was a two-hour drive away. Too far for him to see Chrissy every day. But maybe he could visit her on weekends and holidays.

Katie took a step closer. "I know you might find this difficult to believe right now, but it's going to be okay. You just have to trust in the Lord. He'll help you through this."

Reese snorted. "I'm afraid God and I don't get along too well."

"Maybe it's time for you to change that. If there's one thing I've learned, it's that God never abandons us. Not even when we leave Him. He can help you. I know it. But it's your choice," she suggested bluntly. She paused for several moments, letting her words sink in. She looked at him so intensely that he thought she could see inside his blackened heart.

His jaw went slack, but she turned away. And what could he say to the truth? Nothing. Not when he knew she was dead right. Maybe it was something to think about.

"Lunch is almost ready," she called over her shoulder. "Dad and Chrissy are back. Come inside and have a sandwich with us. You can finish this work later."

He stared after her as she headed toward the motel. She'd ordered him, not asked. Although she'd invited him to dinner that night, he hadn't planned on eating lunch, too. But watching her go, he couldn't help smiling. Motherhood seemed to agree with her. The mousy bookworm was definitely gone.

"I'll be there in just a minute," he said, not trusting his voice to say more.

As she disappeared inside, he thought about the future. Just over two weeks ago, he didn't have a care in the world. Now he'd lost all his friends and had a job offer in a profession he didn't believe he could work anymore, an old girlfriend who resented him for leaving town without a word seven years earlier and a daughter who didn't even know who he was.

No, that wasn't quite right. Katie had never been his girlfriend. Until the night they'd graduated from high school, he'd barely spared her a glance. And though Reese felt the urge to leave town and run far away, he knew he couldn't abandon Katie again. Not this time. He owed her and Chrissy so much. He just didn't know how to breach the walls standing between them or how to fit comfortably in their lives. Maybe he never could.

Chapter Six

Katie turned toward the kitchen table with a large bowl of fruit salad. Her gaze promptly landed on the bouquet of daisies Reese had given her earlier. They sat in a vase of water in the middle of the table. Charlie must have put them there. When he'd returned home with Chrissy a few minutes earlier, they'd immediately noticed the flowers and the gift, where Katie had left them on the counter.

Standing nearby, Charlie poured glasses of milk. Chrissy leaned against the counter, her fingertips lightly brushing over the white bow on the present Reese had brought her. She had zeroed in on it like a heat-seeking missile.

When Charlie turned to put the gallon jug of milk back in the fridge, Katie whisked the flowers out of the way and replaced them with the fruit salad.

Through the kitchen window, she saw Reese cross the backyard toward the motel. His tall, lean figure moved with ease, leather gloves peeking out from where he'd tucked them into one pocket. Dressed in faded blue jeans and work boots, he looked like a day laborer. Strong and tanned. Self-assured. A man's man.

Funny how Reese had been incorporated into the family, as if he belonged here. But he didn't. Not really.

He stepped inside the back door, his eyes meeting hers. He nodded and gave an apologetic smile. "Sorry to keep you waiting. Can you give me a moment to wash up?"

She nodded. "The bathroom is down the hall."

He headed that way. She could hear the spray of water as he washed. Moments later, he returned and glanced at the table. A glint of approval flashed in his eyes.

"Lunch looks good," he said.

Katie turned with a plate of sandwiches and her mouth fell open. Charlie had put the vase of daisies back in the middle of the table, the fruit salad pushed off to the side. She threw her father a disparaging glance, but he merely met her eyes with a challenging lift of his chin.

"What is this?" Chrissy asked, pointing at the gift sitting in front of her.

Reese glanced up as he pulled a chair out to sit down. A mischievous smile curved his handsome mouth. "It looks like a birthday gift to me."

Chrissy shook her head. "It couldn't be a birthday gift. It's wrapped with Easter paper."

"It is?" He peered at the present, as if noticing it for the first time.

"Yes, see the little bunnies." Chrissy pointed out each one, as if it were obvious. Which it was.

He shrugged his too-wide shoulders. "Maybe it's an Easter birthday gift. After all, Easter is when the Lord rose from the tomb to live again. It's the greatest gift He could give us."

Katie blinked. Reese's mother had been a pious woman, but her recalcitrant son had rarely attended church as a teenager. Now hearing him talk about the resurrection seemed odd. She'd assumed he was a hedonist who didn't believe in God. Maybe she was wrong.

"Who is the present for?" Chrissy pressed.

Reese rested his forearms on the table as Charlie took his seat. Katie followed suit, watching and listening to this exchange with interest.

"Doesn't it say?" Reese asked, looking slightly pleased by this dialogue.

Chrissy picked up the gaily wrapped gift and checked it over twice. "No, there's no card, but Mommy said you brought it for me."

"Yes, it's for you," he said.

Her forehead crinkled in puzzlement. "But what for?"

"Your birthday, of course."

"But it's not my birthday."

He tilted his head to one side, pretending to be confused. Lifting a hand, he scratched his head. "It's not? That's funny. I was almost certain it was your birthday. But I guess I made a mistake and will just have to take it back to the store."

Chrissy gasped and Charlie chuckled with amusement.

"No, don't take it back," she pleaded. "Can't I open it now? Please."

Katie didn't say a word. She quietly dished up fruit salad and placed a chicken salad sandwich on her daughter's plate. A flash of memory filled her mind of Reese as a kid, teasing an attractive girl in their high school gymnasium. He'd been charming and playful just like now. Seeing him like this with her daughter reminded Katie that he was Chrissy's father. That he'd never teased her this way. Never been charming toward her. Never really cared.

Except for the flowers he'd given her today.

A rattle of dishes brought Charlie's head up and he

looked in her direction. Katie realized she was trembling, and she sat back, gazing at her plate as she folded her hands in her lap. Pretending that nothing was wrong. Pretending that this was a normal day like any other. But it wasn't.

"You can open the gift, if it's all right with your mom," Reese said.

Everyone turned and looked at Katie. Her face heated up like road flares, but she didn't trust her voice to speak. She merely nodded.

With a cry of delight, Chrissy carefully removed the white bow from the present and set it aside. Then she shredded the paper. Once she hit the plethora of tape Reese had used to seal the ends, she had trouble getting the box open. Charlie, who was sitting nearest to her, assisted with a flick of his long fingers.

Chrissy lifted the narrow flap and then gasped. "Look!"

Katie sat up straighter, wondering what it could be.

Ever so gently, Chrissy reached inside the box and removed a wooden case. She raised the lid and reached inside, then held up a shiny silver compass. An expensive one, if Katie was any judge. She glanced at Reese, thinking he was crazy to buy something so delicate for a six-year-old.

"Wow! My very own compass," Chrissy cried as she held it reverently in her hands. "Now I can find my true north all by myself."

"That's right. I hope you like it," Reese said.

"I love it." Chrissy beamed a happy smile.

"Good. I'm glad." Reese smiled, too.

"What do you say, Chrissy?" Katie prompted in a soft voice.

"Thank you. Thank you so, so, so much," the girl replied.

"You're welcome, sweetheart. Maybe after lunch, I can teach you how to use it," Reese said.

"Yes. I'd love that more than anything in the whole wide world," Chrissy said.

Charlie grunted in approval, but Katie sat there in stunned silence. She felt as though her ears were clogged, like she was underwater. Of all the gifts Katie had bought her daughter, Chrissy had never reacted like this. It was a compass, not a dolly. Not a puzzle or coloring books or something a little girl might like. And yet, from Chrissy's reaction, you would have thought it was the most precious gift she'd ever received.

Katie made a pretense of passing a plate of carrot and celery sticks to Charlie. As he led the four of them in a blessing on the food, she bowed her head, but her eyes remained open. She couldn't concentrate. Couldn't get used to the idea of Reese being here in their lives. And yet it felt as though he'd always been here. But he hadn't. Not once.

"You want some chips?" Charlie asked, holding a basket of barbecue potato chips toward her.

She shook her head, her thoughts scattering. Picking up her fork, she forced herself to spear a chunk of watermelon and put it in her mouth. While Chrissy and Reese chatted about the compass, Katie could feel her father's gaze resting on her like a ten-ton sledge. She couldn't pretend she was happy about this situation. Not when she knew how Reese had always felt about her. He'd been bushwhacked with the news that he had a child.

She steeled her heart, reminding herself why she'd told him the truth. This was about Chrissy, meeting her daddy and making her happy. Otherwise, Reese wouldn't be here now. This had nothing to do with the adults in the room. He didn't care about Katie herself. Not one bit. And that hurt most of all.

Reese barely tasted his lunch. Looking around the table, he felt odd and out of place. Until he'd returned to town, he'd never had this experience before. Sitting at the table, having a simple meal as happy chatter flowed around him. Like a real family. And yet he sensed that Katie wasn't happy.

He passed her the fruit salad, even though she'd barely touched what she already had on her plate. She was way too quiet and he wanted to engage her in conversation.

As she took the bowl, their gazes met. Her fingers brushed against his, her skin warm and smooth. Her cheeks were pink, her eyes wide with uncertainty. A strand of hair stuck to her forehead. She reached up and brushed it away, looking like the naive, uncertain girl he used to know.

She broke eye contact, as though she couldn't stand to look at him. He realized she must still resent him. He couldn't blame her. He'd taken her for granted all those years ago. She'd trusted him then, but he'd betrayed her. And now, a part of him wanted to regain that trust. To regain her affection and admiration. But he wasn't sure how.

Twenty minutes later, he was outside in the back of the motel, crouched beside Chrissy as they had a brief compass lesson. He'd tried to help clear the table, but the girl had been antsy with excitement and Katie had insisted he go. He'd set his plate in the sink, then followed Chrissy outside as she pulled on his hand.

"See that field over there?" Reese pointed to a vacant

lot surrounded by a barbed wire fence that bordered the back of the motel.

"Yes." Chrissy looked up, her hair gleaming in the sunshine.

"Can you tell me what direction it's in?" he asked.

Chrissy studied the compass for several moments, her forehead furrowed. Then she answered with a decisive nod of her head. "West."

"That's right. And what about the motel? What direction is it?"

Another pause. "East."

"Very good. Maybe in a day or two, you can come up to Cove Mountain and I'll take you into the forest to practice your technique. It's harder when you're surrounded by thick vegetation and can't see the sun's position."

"You're my daddy, huh?"

Reese jerked his head up and stared at the child. Her words struck him like a physical blow to the chest. How had she found out? He'd thought he and Katie were going to tell her together. But maybe Katie had decided to have *the talk* without him, kind of as a way to break the ice and see how Chrissy took the news.

"How...how would you know?" he asked, feeling a bit queasy.

Chrissy shrugged and looked down at the compass, seeming suddenly shy. "I've got your eyes. Plus Mommy has a picture of you in her sock drawer, from when you graduated from high school. She doesn't know, but I sneak and look at it all the time. She doesn't have pictures of any other boys, so I know it's special to her."

Katie had a picture of him in her sock drawer? That was surprising news. And he wondered how she had acquired it. He couldn't remember giving her one. But since she had Chrissy, he could understand why she'd obtained a picture to keep for the little girl. Then another thought occurred to him. Maybe she kept the picture for herself. And the idea that she cared enough about him to hold on to his picture touched Reese's heart like nothing else could.

It was on the tip of his tongue to deny it. Katie obviously hadn't told Chrissy the truth yet, but since the girl had come to the correct assumption on her own, he couldn't ignore it, nor would he lie. With his upbringing, he despised secrets and lies more than anything. But he felt suddenly clumsy and inadequate. Of all the men who should be this bright little girl's father, why did it get to be him? He wasn't father material. In fact, he'd never thought he'd ever settle down and have a family of his own. His father had been a miserable failure. Reese had grown up thinking that families were a means of torture and pain. Besides, maybe Chrissy wouldn't like him. Maybe she and Katie deserved better than him.

"Yes, I'm your father. Is that all right?" he asked.

"Sure. You don't get to pick your parents."

So true. She said the words as though it was no big deal, but it was to him. Before he'd known the truth, it hadn't mattered. Now it did. People were counting on him. He wasn't alone anymore. Maybe his relationship with Katie and Chrissy was odd and dysfunctional right now, but they were his. Weren't they?

"If you were a stranger, I couldn't go off into the woods with you to learn how to use the compass. But since you're my daddy, I can trust you," she said.

No! No! he wanted to yell. No one could trust him. Except for his employer, he'd let everyone else down. His mother, teachers, Katie and numerous other girlfriends. He had no lasting relationships. Nothing binding. But hearing about this child's confidence in him made him feel funny inside. Like he should try to be better for her. And better for Katie, too.

"Chrissy."

They both looked up. Charlie was hobbling toward them, tugging a pair of leather gloves onto his big hands.

"Yes, Papa?" she said.

"Your mommy wants you to go inside and work on your school assignments now. It's time for Reese and me to finish the roof on the shed," Charlie said.

"Okay, Papa." The girl embraced her grandpa, then hugged Reese. She collected her compass and hurried toward the house.

Leaving Reese alone with Katie's father. Reese could feel the man's gaze boring into him like a high-speed drill.

"Show me what you've accomplished." Charlie gestured toward the shed.

Whew! That broke the ice. Katie had said that Charlie knew Reese was Chrissy's father, and he couldn't help wondering how that made the man feel. If Chrissy grew up and someone got her pregnant, then abandoned her, Reese would want to hunt the guy down and throttle him. He definitely had to give Charlie credit for maintaining his temper.

Grateful for the distraction of work, Reese stood and hurried over to the ladder. He shimmied up in record time, with Charlie following at a more cumbersome speed.

Reese eyed the older man dubiously. "Are you sure you want to help? Katie said she doesn't want you up on the roof."

Charlie scooted his hips over, resting his weight on the beams of lumber. "I'll go crazy if I sit around doing nothing all day long."

Reese didn't argue. He felt the same way, hence his desire to help.

The two men worked together for some time, making fast progress. Charlie couldn't walk well, but he could sure wield a hammer.

"Are you thinking about taking Sean Nash up on his job offer?" he asked after a while.

Reese tensed. "You know about that?"

Charlie didn't pause in his hammering, speaking between each strike of the nail. "He mentioned it to me."

"I'm not really interested in fighting fires right now," Reese said.

Charlie held two roofing nails between his lips. Reaching up, he retrieved one, put it in place and drove it into the shingle with one sharp smack. "What do you want to do, then?"

Reese stared at his hammer. "I thought I'd be a firefighter for the rest of my life. Now I don't think I can do it anymore."

A long silence followed. "No need to think about it right now. Give yourself time to heal. The Lord will let you know what you should do."

Reese doubted it but didn't say so.

"I guess Katie told you about Chrissy, huh?" Charlie asked.

Reese didn't pretend not to understand. "Yeah, she told me."

Charlie worked for a few moments, hammering away. "Katie had a lot of opportunities when she graduated from high school. Scholarships. Education. A great career doing something she loved. She could have become anything she wanted."

"Yes, I know that, sir." Reese wasn't sure where the man was going with this.

"Imagine how she felt when she discovered she was pregnant and the father had left town," Charlie continued.

"I didn't know about the baby, sir. I never abandoned her."

Charlie held his hammer in midair as he looked up and met Reese's eyes. "So, you just used her, then left town, is that it?"

Reese felt a sinking in his heart. "I…I didn't mean to use her, sir. I'm sorry. I was young and stupid."

"You might want to tell Katie that. And I hope you've learned a few things since then." Charlie started hammering again.

"She never told me about the baby, or I would have been here," Reese said.

Charlie paused, his eyes narrowed on Reese's face, as though he was seeking the truth. "Would you?"

"Yes, sir. If I'd known she was carrying my child, I would have been by her side."

But Reese wasn't so sure. His own father had been such a disappointment. Drunken rages. Lashing out at Reese and his mother when they weren't expecting it. The bruises and marks Reese couldn't explain to his teachers at school. And yet, no one had done a thing to help. The abuse had made him the man he'd become, but he was not going to allow that to happen to his child. No, sirree. He'd never planned to have a child of his own, but now that he did, he wanted to protect her. And that meant that her mother had to be all right, too. Chrissy's well-being depended, to a great extent, on Katie's happiness.

"Chrissy knows, too," Reese said.

Charlie whipped his head up. "How?"

He shrugged. "Apparently Katie has a picture of me stashed in her sock drawer. Chrissy found it when she was snooping around."

Charlie laughed and shook his head. "Sometimes that little girl is too smart for her own good."

"You got that right," Reese said.

They worked for a few minutes more, then Reese asked a question of his own. "Why didn't Katie give the baby up so she could go to college?"

Charlie thought about that for a moment. "That wasn't an option for Katie. She's fiercely loyal. There was no way she was about to turn her back on her own child."

Reese wished his father had been that protective of him and his mother. Under the circumstances, his mom had done her best, but a part of Reese couldn't help wishing she had left his dad and taken him away somewhere they could be free of the abuse. As a child, he'd tried to intercede when his father used his fists on his mother. But what could a young kid do against a tall, strong man? Not much. He'd left as soon as he graduated from high school.

"Katie's been taking some online classes," Charlie said. "Once Chrissy starts first grade, she's hoping to drive into Reno a couple days per week so she can take classes at the university. I'd have to help out with Chrissy, of course, but it's important for Katie to go to school. I've encouraged her to give up her job at the newspaper office and go to school full-time."

Reese picked up his hammer and several nails. "She should do it."

"She'd need help with Chrissy. I do what I can, but I'm getting older. I can't always leave the motel desk to get Chrissy from school, but we'll figure it out some way," Charlie continued.

What was he saying? Reese wasn't sure.

Charlie was the kind of dad Reese wished that he'd had when he was growing up. But raising Chrissy was not Charlie's job. He was her grandpa, not her father.

Chrissy was Reese's responsibility. But he couldn't stay here indefinitely. At some point, he'd have to leave town to find employment.

"I just wish Katie had told me years earlier," Reese said.

Charlie nodded, speaking in a matter-of-fact voice. "Well, she didn't. I figure you now have two choices. You can be angry about it, or you can accept it and move on from here and be happy."

Reese froze. Happy? "What do you mean?"

"Chrissy needs a daddy. I've done my best to fill that need, but I'm still just her grandpa. You can make a big difference in that little girl's life. You can make a big difference in Katie's life, too. You're young and strong, with your future ahead of you. It's just a matter of deciding what you really want and then going for it. It's up to you."

"I see." Reese bowed his head, thinking this over. He had no idea what he wanted anymore. He'd never thought that far ahead.

Charlie placed his hand on Reese's shoulder. "You're not your father, Reese. You can choose to be a better man."

The words were said very quietly. Charlie didn't wait for a response but turned and reached for another shingle. He set it in place, then nailed it down tight.

Reese worked beside him in silence, his thoughts in turmoil. He could choose to be different than his father. He'd lived his life free as a whirlwind, doing exactly what he pleased. Now his freedom no longer held as much appeal. Finding out that he had a child had scared him to death. At first. But since he'd been getting to know Chrissy, he realized he kind of liked having a little girl. A lot. But what about Katie?

When he'd given her the bouquet of daisies, she'd

looked repulsed. And when Chrissy had opened his gift, Reese had seen the anger in Katie's eyes. Her lips had tightened into a prim line. She didn't approve. No doubt, she wished Chrissy's father was anyone but him. And it occurred to him that he and Katie had switched places in a way. During high school, he'd been aware that she had a horrible crush on him. Most girls did. He'd been good-looking, athletic, charming, and he knew it. Given her mousy looks, he'd barely spared Katie a second glance.

In spite of her mistakes, she'd held her head up and raised their daughter alone. Now the prodigal son had returned. Humble and lost. Needing a refuge from the world. A sinner who needed repentance in the worst way. But no matter what he did to make things right, he wasn't sure he could ever win Katie's forgiveness or trust.

Chapter Seven

"You sure you want to help wash the dishes?" Katie said.

Standing in front of the kitchen sink, she dipped her hands into the hot, sudsy water and swiped the dishcloth over a plate. Just before dinner, Charlie had told her that Chrissy had already guessed Reese was her father. Because of a picture Katie kept in her drawer. It was Reese's senior picture and she'd gotten it from the high school. She didn't even know why she'd kept it all this time. But now, Katie understood why Chrissy had taken to Reese so fast. She'd known he was her father from the moment they first met. And there was nothing Chrissy wanted more than to have her daddy in her life.

"I don't mind washing dishes, if you'd like. Or I can dry. I'm pretty good at KP duty," Reese said.

He stood beside her, his arm brushing against her shoulder. She resisted the urge to look up at him. "KP duty?"

"Kitchen patrol." He shrugged his impossibly broad shoulders, then reached past her for a dish towel. "Since you've already got your hands in the sink, how about if I dry?"

She doubted he'd ever washed dishes as a teenager. "Where did you learn KP duty?"

"My hotshot crew."

He bumped against her and she scrunched her shoulders, drawing back. She tried to pretend his presence didn't affect her. That she didn't want to gaze into his eyes and study the contours of his face.

"I thought you fought fires with your crew," she said, trying to keep her voice calm.

"I did, among other things. When we were on the fire line, our meals were prepared for us by a caterer."

She nodded. "Yes, when we've got a fire in the local area, Megan Marshall prepares meals from her restaurant for the hand crews."

"When my hotshot crew was at our home base, we took turns preparing a number of our meals. I frequently had KP duty. And believe it or not, I make a mean pot roast."

She laughed. "Maybe I'll let you make Sunday dinner for us. You might be able to teach me a thing or two."

"I might." He chuckled, his eyes twinkling. But then he went very quiet and a deep sadness settled across his face.

She rinsed a glass and reached across him to set it in the dish drain. "Are you okay?"

"Yeah. It's just hard to talk about my friends. Sometimes I forget they're all gone, and I miss them." He picked up the glass and dried it, his voice sounding hoarse with emotion.

Something painful wrenched inside Katie. She'd spent the last seven years believing that Reese didn't care about anyone but himself. That he was lazy, selfish and heartless.

"From what I've heard on the news, you're blessed to

be alive." She didn't want to care about this man and his troubles, yet she couldn't seem to help it.

He snorted. "I wouldn't call it blessed. In many ways, I feel ostracized."

"Why do you say that?" She tilted her head and gave him a sidelong glance as she handed him a plate. He dried it with several quick swipes of the towel, then set it on the counter with the other clean dishes.

"I'm the only one that survived," he said in a low, thoughtful voice. "And I don't think it should have been that way. I should have died, too. I was the only one without a family. Each of my buddies had people back at home waiting for their return, yet I'm the only one who got out of there alive."

She heard the note of pain in his voice. She wasn't sure how to respond but knew she had to say something.

"I know what it feels like to think your life is ruined," she said. "That you can never make it right again. But you can't stop believing. You can never quit trying."

He gave an ugly scoff. "People like me are beyond repair."

"Reese, just because your crew died doesn't mean the Lord didn't hear your prayers," she said. "He saved you, didn't He? He knows this isn't all there is to life and He sees the bigger picture of eternity. You shouldn't give up on Him. In fact, maybe you're looking at this all wrong."

He shifted his weight. "How so?"

"Maybe you should cherish this second chance you've been given and use it to do a lot of good in the world. To honor the memory of your friends who died."

He jerked his head toward her but didn't respond. His dark eyebrows drew together in a deep, thoughtful frown. It hurt her to think that he didn't believe in the Lord. That he didn't believe in anything. But she sensed that it wasn't so much that Reese didn't believe, but rather that he was angry at God. It rattled her that he was confiding in her. These were the poignant things Tom Klarch wanted her to write about. And she decided then that she would put it all down on paper, capture it while the emotions were fresh. But the story would never be published unless Reese gave his go-ahead.

She tried to think of something else to talk about. Something less morbid. But what came out next startled her.

"Have you got a girlfriend?" she asked, unable to stop herself. She'd been wondering about this ever since she'd told him he was Chrissy's father. She had to know if there was a woman in his life that she'd have to deal with. After all, he might have other children, too. Katie had no idea how complicated this situation might get. She just hoped and prayed she was up to the challenge.

Reese couldn't help smiling with amusement. He hadn't expected Katie's question and wondered if he imagined a tinge of jealousy in her voice.

"Why do you ask? Are you in the market?"

Color flooded her face. "Of course not. I was just wondering, in case you want to introduce her to Chrissy."

He laughed. "No, I don't have anyone. I rarely date, I've never been married and I have no other children that I know about."

She blinked at him, saw that he was teasing her, then smiled. It wasn't a laughing matter, especially since she'd kept Chrissy a secret from him, but he was glad they could find a little bit of humor in their situation. Laughter was good medicine for them.

He leaned his hip against the counter and flipped the

dish towel over his shoulder. "Why are you so interested in my private life?"

"I…I was just wondering if my daughter had any brothers and sisters."

Reese could accept that. He'd been gone a long time. If he was going to build a relationship with his daughter, then Katie had a right to know what to expect from him. But he was telling the truth. He used to drink and party, but he'd felt too insecure to develop a lasting relationship with a woman. He was too afraid of becoming abusive like his father.

One day, Katie might settle down with another man. Reese told himself that he didn't care. Up until the fire, he'd been content with his life and didn't need a wife or family to make him happy. He'd be relieved when it was time to move on. Wouldn't he? So why did the thought of never seeing Katie again leave him feeling empty inside?

His heart gave a powerful surge and he looked away. "I'm not the kind of man who should ever fall in love."

"Why do you believe that?" she pressed.

"Because if I ever marry, I'll only hurt my wife, the way my father hurt my mother and me. And I don't want that."

The confession slipped out so easily. And the moment he said the words, he regretted them. Katie was much too easy to talk to and he didn't like confiding such private things to her. It exposed too much of his heart, and he'd learned from sad experience not to trust easily. If you didn't trust, then you didn't get hurt. It was that simple.

"You're not your father, Reese," she said.

"No, I haven't had a drink in six years. But I'm still my father's son. I don't want to take the chance that I'll become an abuser, so I don't plan to ever get hitched. It's best that I play it safe."

"I'm sorry. I didn't mean to get so personal." Her voice sounded deflated.

"Well, now you know." He took the dishcloth from her, wrung it out and turned away to wipe down the counters. It was a good diversion and gave him the opportunity to do something besides look at her beautiful profile.

He wanted to be better than his father, but he also feared that his dad still lived within him. That he would hurt anyone he loved. And so he couldn't fall in love. Not ever.

"What are your plans for the next few days?" she asked.

He shrugged. "I hadn't really thought about it. Why?"

"If you're interested, you could help with a service project I've been working on over at Elsa Watkins's house. It would involve some simple yard work and a few repairs, nothing too strenuous."

His interest was piqued. "I think you mentioned that earlier."

"Yes. I've been making some visits, to find out what her needs might be."

He pretended a shudder. "I'm afraid Mrs. Watkins wouldn't want me in her home."

Katie paused. "I almost forgot. You and your gang of friends got drunk and ripped out her tomato plants and smashed the prize watermelons she was planning to enter in the county fair."

He cringed at her graphic description. "Yes, and I regret it."

She laughed. "I suspect Mrs. Watkins regrets it, too. But maybe it's time for you to compensate. And what better way than to help clean up her yard? She's been having a rather difficult time since her husband died. She's got a bad hip and can't move without a walker. She can't even mow her own lawn anymore."

Hmm. Maybe Katie was right. Maybe it was time he made amends for what he'd done. And not just for Mrs. Watkins's garden. He owed apologies to numerous people in town. Some of them might reject his contrition, but he had to try. He sensed that was the only way he could ever be right with the world. Providing service to those people he had wronged was certainly better than spending his days holed up at the cabin in boredom. But the more he was seen out in public, the more chance the media might find him again. That was the chance he'd have to take.

"Let me think about it," he said, not wanting to confess his thoughts to her.

She pursed her lips in a doubtful expression. "Whatever."

She obviously didn't believe he cared or that he wanted to help. But he did. And that realization surprised him.

He looked out the window and saw that it was dark. He'd spent almost the entire day here and was surprised that he'd enjoyed every minute of it. But now the clock on the wall said it was half past nine. Chrissy had already gone to bed. The summer sky twinkled with a zillion stars; the air from the open window was scented with honeysuckle. Time to go home and sleep, if he could.

"I guess I'll be going," he said.

"Yes, you don't want to have an accident on your way home." She hung the dish towel on the stove door handle.

Home. He never thought he would consider a cabin on Cove Mountain as his home, but he felt more comfortable there and in this motel than any place he'd ever lived.

"I'll walk you out." She led the way, her bare feet padding across the linoleum floor.

Outside, the lights in the parking lot gleamed brightly, chasing away the dim shadows. Katie stood on the back steps and folded her arms, scrunching her shoulders against the slight chill in the air.

"It's a bit cold out. Go in." He jutted his chin toward the screen door.

"Let me know when you'd like to see Chrissy again," she said.

"I will." He waved as he climbed into his borrowed truck.

He started up the engine, flipped on the headlights and pulled out of the garage. As he drove down the narrow alley, he glanced in the rearview mirror. Katie stood right where he'd left her, her face pale in the shadows of the building. And for some crazy reason, he wished he didn't have to leave.

Chapter Eight

Three days later, Katie loaded Chrissy into her car and drove toward Elsa Watkins's home. She'd promised the elderly widow that she'd do some yard work for her today. Weed the flower beds and plant some petunias. Now that school was out for summer break, it'd be a fun mother-daughter outing, where she could have some time alone with Chrissy to chat. Even though Chrissy knew Reese was her father, Katie wanted to find out what her daughter was thinking, and explain a few things to her.

As they drove down Main Street, Chrissy sat in the back, buckled into her booster seat. Katie had pulled the girl's hair into two long ponytails, one on each side of her head. Chrissy gazed out the window, her pert nose held high. Glancing in her rearview mirror, Katie saw that her daughter looked so guileless and pure that it brought a sweet ache to Katie's chest. She'd do anything to protect her child. She was wondering how to broach the subject on her mind when Chrissy asked a blunt question.

"Why didn't you marry my daddy?"

Katie tried to swallow, but her throat felt as though a balled-up sheet of sandpaper were lodged there. Okay, here it was. The moment of truth. But Katie hadn't expected this particular question.

"I, um… He never asked me," Katie said.

"Why not?"

She inwardly groaned. These were surprisingly difficult questions. They forced her to face up to the truth. She didn't want to lie to her child, but it hurt to say the next words.

"He didn't love me."

Chrissy's forehead furrowed. "But you had me."

"Yes, we did." Katie picked her words carefully, gazing at her child in the rearview mirror.

"Did you love him?" Chrissy sat forward and looked at her, her big green eyes so wide and innocent.

"Yes, I did," she answered honestly. "At least, at the time I did."

"But not anymore?"

"I…I love him for giving me you," Katie said.

That was true enough. Of all the rotten things Reese had done during high school, at least he'd given her a beautiful daughter to cherish. She would always love and appreciate him for that.

"We were awfully young at the time, sweetums. We were inexperienced and naive and we made a…" Katie was about to say the word *mistake* but stopped herself just in time. No, no! She didn't want Chrissy to ever believe she was a mistake, because she wasn't.

"We made a choice not to marry. Now your father is here in town, and I hope you two can become great friends," Katie said, trying to recover her wits.

How could she tell her daughter that she'd been trusting and stupid and never should have gone with Reese that fateful night? But if she hadn't, she wouldn't have

Chrissy now. And she could never regret having her little girl. Not ever.

"Why didn't you tell me about my daddy?" Chrissy asked.

"I was waiting until you were older."

"But I'm a big girl now. I can understand these things," Chrissy said.

Katie almost laughed. Sitting there in the car, her six-year-old daughter looked so self-assured and grown-up. And yet Katie knew better. It'd be so easy to hurt this little girl. To destroy her feelings of security and trust. And Katie didn't want that.

"Yes, I think you're right. You're growing up so fast and it's time you knew about your dad," Katie said.

"I like Reese a lot. I'm glad he's my daddy. But I think he's lonely. He needs us," Chrissy said.

How intuitive. And yet Katie doubted he needed anyone. A part of her thought it served Reese right if he was lonely. He'd chosen his life. She didn't owe him anything. And soon, he'd leave town again. He'd walk right out of their lives the way he'd done before. Without looking back.

They passed the small cemetery on the edge of town. Without thinking about it, Katie glanced to the south side, where a large willow tree swayed protectively over her mother's grave. A blue sedan was parked along the curb of the street. She didn't recognize the vehicle. A trail of smoke rose from the open car window. Someone sitting and smoking. A man? Katie wasn't sure.

In the quick moments before she passed the car, she saw him raise an arm to shield his eyes from the bright sunlight…or to hide his identity. Katie got the impression he didn't want to be seen.

"Look! There's Daddy," Chrissy cried, pointing to the other side of the street.

Sure enough, Reese stood in Mrs. Watkins's yard just off the main road. What was he doing there?

As she pulled into the graveled driveway, Katie glanced at the white frame house with russet trim. She noticed that the elderly widow sat in a wicker chair on the front porch, her walker beside her. She was calmly watching as Reese leaned over her front gate with a hammer. A red toolbox rested on the ground beside his booted feet. He wore leather gloves, faded blue jeans and a black T-shirt that hugged his strong biceps. He had a baseball cap pulled low over his forehead, as though he didn't want to be recognized. But Katie would have known him anywhere. His masculine stance. The tilt of his head.

Considering the damage he'd done to Mrs. Watkins's garden years earlier, Katie thought he was brave to come around here now. But the woman didn't look upset. She smiled and waved as Katie and Chrissy got out of their car.

Reese looked up and saw them. "Hi, there."

"Hello," Katie returned.

"I'm gonna help rake leaves," Chrissy said as she tugged on the oversize cloth gardening gloves Katie had loaned her.

"You are, huh?" Reese set his hammer aside and smiled at the girl.

"Yoo-hoo. You're too late, I'm afraid." Mrs. Watkins waved to draw their attention.

"Hi, Mrs. Watkins. How are you today?" Katie asked, walking up onto the porch to give her a hug. A tray with a half-empty jug of lemonade and a few remaining chocolate chip cookies sat on the table beside her chair.

"I'm just great, honey. Thanks for coming over."

"May I have a cookie, please?" Chrissy asked.

"Of course you can," Mrs. Watkins said.

While Chrissy snatched up a treat and started munching away, the woman clasped the arms of her walker and rose slowly to her feet. Katie helped her.

"Do you know, this young man has been working here all morning. Just look at what he's accomplished." She jutted her chin toward Reese, then gestured to her yard.

Katie's gaze scanned the tidy piles of dried leaves all ready to be bagged up, the pruned bushes and the flower beds neatly weeded and raked. Her nose twitched at the smell of fresh paint. She looked at the front door, which was slightly ajar and shimmered with a new coat of creamy gold. It was late in the season to be raking leaves; the chore should have been done weeks earlier. The yellow lawn needed watering badly. But it boggled Katie's mind that Reese had come over here and done all this work by himself.

Noticing that Mrs. Watkins was now trying to sit down again, Katie reached out to fluff the pillows on the porch swing and helped the lady get comfortable.

"Thank you, dear."

"You're welcome." Katie smiled sweetly, wishing her own mother were still here to dote on.

"Oh, no! Now we can't rake the leaves. It's already done." Chrissy placed her little hands on her hips, pursed her lips and gazed at the yard with disappointment.

Reese lifted one foot to rest against the bottom step of the porch and leaned against the handrail. He studied the yard for a moment, then glanced at his daughter. "Maybe not, but do you know what the next best thing to raking up leaves is?"

She shook her head, her frown firmly in place.

"Jumping in the piles." He tugged on Chrissy's arm to

get her to follow him. When she did, he tossed an armful of dried leaves at the girl.

At first, Chrissy looked shocked. She stared at Reese and blinked. Katie hurried down the stairs, hoping the day didn't end in tears.

With a squeal of delight, Chrissy scooped up as many leaves as possible and threw them right back at Reese. And before Katie knew what was happening, her daughter was chasing the tall man around the yard, frolicking in the leaves, spreading them around the grass.

"Oh, dear," Mrs. Watkins murmured as she saw her tidy yard turned back into a mess.

"Don't worry. We'll clean it up again," Katie assured her.

She smiled. "Oh, thank you, dear. You should join in and have fun, then."

"I don't think…" Katie turned and found a bunch of crackling leaves being thrown in her face by Chrissy.

"Hey!" she cried, brushing at her clothes. It did no good. She found another pile of leaves dropped over her head by Reese. They fell harmlessly around her feet, but a few clung to her hair and clothes.

She eyed her daughter and the man, wondering how to react. And then she decided to give as good as she got.

"All right, you two. You're asking for it." She scooped up a big armful and tossed it at them. The two instigators scattered, their laughter filling the air. Reese pulled the girl with him, scurrying behind a tall tree for cover.

"Don't think you can hide from me!" Katie laughed as she tore after them.

Chrissy popped out and tossed more leaves. Katie scooped up her daughter and twirled her around. The girl's giggles bubbled up as they spun until they were both dizzy.

Katie found herself knocked backward into a soft pile of leaves. And then…

"Oof!"

A heavy weight landed near her. Looking up, she found Reese lying beside her, his eyes wide with surprise. Chrissy stood over them, chortling hysterically. The girl had obviously knocked him down, too, but only because he let her. Chrissy wasn't finished yet. She jumped on top of them, rolling, kicking at the leaves, having a blast. Katie couldn't help herself; she laughed and laughed. And it felt so good. So normal and fun.

Reese's deep chuckles rumbled from his chest. He threw leaves at Chrissy and the child buried her face against his chest.

"Don't get me! Don't get me," she cried. Which meant just the opposite—she wanted him to get her.

Reese obliged, tickling her, then holding her tight. "That'll teach you to take on your mom and dad."

Katie jerked. She glanced toward the porch. Mrs. Watkins was laughing, too, showing no sign that she'd overheard Reese's comment.

Chrissy's muffled reply was indistinguishable.

Katie turned, her face no more than a hand's breadth away from Reese. Their gazes locked. She caught his scent, an earthy smell of spicy aftershave, rich loamy soil and sawdust. She felt drawn to him, like the tide to the shore. Her thoughts scattered and she couldn't think about anything but him. He lifted a hand to squeeze her arm. She felt lost in his smile. Mesmerized as he leaned nearer. And then…

Chrissy popped up between them, breaking the moment. "Hey, I'm hungry. Can we go to Rocklin and get something to eat?"

Katie quickly came to her feet, her face heating up

like road flares. This had gotten out of hand. She hadn't meant to forget herself. She must be more careful.

"Um, sure. I'll even buy. After we clean up this mess." Reese stood and rested his hands on his hips. He looked around, assessing the damage.

"Can we, Mom? Please?" the child begged.

What should she say? She'd never seen her daughter this happy and animated. But if they were seen with Reese at the restaurant, people might get the wrong impression. Yet she didn't want to dispel her daughter's joy. Chrissy had waited over six years to be with her father. The girl needed this time with him.

"Okay, but after we've finished our work," Katie conceded.

"It's not too bad," Reese said. "If we pitch in together, we can get it done quickly."

They did so, and Chrissy had never worked so hard. An hour later, they had all the dried leaves bagged up and Reese had fertilized and mowed the lawn. He then turned on the sprinklers.

"Oh, thank you," Mrs. Watkins exclaimed, her gray eyes twinkling. "You've done so much for me. But I mostly enjoyed having laughter in my yard again. You make such a cute couple. I hope you'll come back and visit me often."

"Chrissy and I will definitely visit you again," Katie said, but she didn't want to give the woman the wrong idea. She was not together with Reese. She never would be.

"It was my pleasure to help," he said.

Katie caught the note of earnestness in his voice. She couldn't deny that he'd worked hard.

Mrs. Watkins braced her hands on her walker and stood shakily. Reese hurried to assist, patiently helping her hobble over to her front door. The woman paused there, resting a hand on his arm.

"I'm so glad you've changed, son. I was worried about you when you were young. But I think Joy would be proud of the man you've become," the woman said.

Joy. Reese's mother.

"Hey! My middle name is Joy," Chrissy said, her nose crinkling.

Katie inwardly cringed. She hadn't yet explained to Chrissy that she'd been named after her father's mother.

Mrs. Watkins glanced at the little girl, then at Reese. The woman assessed the two and Katie hoped she didn't notice the similarities. Katie wasn't ready for everyone in town to know that he was Chrissy's father.

Reese's face flushed red and he looked away, as though he were suddenly overcome by emotion. He must be feeling embarrassed, too. "Thanks, ma'am."

"Come on, Chrissy. We've got to go," Katie called, relieved when the little girl came running.

Katie stepped away with misgivings. Cleaning up an elderly woman's yard was one single incident. It didn't necessarily mean that Reese had changed. But she had to admit she was genuinely surprised by this new side she was viewing. She no longer knew what to believe about him.

Reese opened the door to Rocklin Diner and held it as Katie and Chrissy stepped inside. The bell tinkled gaily as they looked around for a place to sit. Reese's stomach rumbled. It was late afternoon and the homemade chocolate chip cookies and lemonade Mrs. Watkins had given him had long ago worn off.

The air smelled of basil, fried chicken and cinnamon. Reese's mouth watered. He glanced at his daughter and noticed a pair of binoculars hanging around her neck. An odd item for a child her age to be wearing. She must have picked them up in her mom's car.

"But Papa's not here with us. What will he eat for dinner?" Chrissy asked her mother.

"I'll order a meal to take home to him," Katie said with a smile.

Reese liked that Chrissy was so considerate of other people, and he again thought that Katie had done a good job raising their child.

He hesitated, glancing around the diner to make sure no members of the media were there. He hadn't seen any reporters for a couple days. He'd had an exceptionally wonderful afternoon and didn't want anything to spoil it. Helping Mrs. Watkins with all the work she needed done had given him a warm glow that filled his chest. It made him feel good. And laughing with Chrissy and Katie had pulled his life into focus. For a short time, he'd felt as though his future couldn't get any brighter. That all was right with the world. He felt…happy. And yet it was more than that. A peaceful feeling he couldn't explain. Like he'd done something good by cleaning up Mrs. Watkins's yard. Something that really made a difference for someone else.

Several people sat in the booths, but he recognized only two. Harry and Caroline Carter, whose fence Reese and his friends had crashed into years earlier when they were driving home from a party late one night. They'd all been drinking heavily, but he'd been driving the car.

"Hi, Reese." Harry immediately stood and reached out to clasp his hand. Caroline smiled pleasantly.

"Hello, sir. Mrs. Carter." Reese nodded at them both, conscious of Katie standing nearby. He pulled the rim of his baseball cap down to hide his face, hoping no one else noticed him.

"It sure was nice of you to help us out yesterday," Harry said.

"My pleasure. How is your truck running?" Reese spoke low, trying not to attract attention.

"Like a top. Where did you learn to work on engines?" Harry asked.

Reese felt Chrissy take his hand. The instinct rose up in him to pull away. His own father never held his hand or showed him affection, especially not in public. But Reese didn't want to treat his child the way his father had treated him. He couldn't push her away. Conscious of Katie watching him like a protective momma grizzly, he tightened his fingers around Chrissy's and held on tight enough to let her know he was delighted to have her near.

"I did a lot of engine work on my hotshot crew. Whenever one of our chain saws or trucks broke down, they always brought it to me first. I seem to have a knack for it," he said.

And that was when something critical dawned on him. When his father wasn't drinking, he'd worked as a mechanic. In a rush, Reese remembered numerous times throughout his life when he'd overheard his father talking about how to fix a car problem, or he'd looked over his father's shoulder as he was working on an engine. Reese had grown up knowing how to change the oil, how to change the brake pads and how to flush the coolant out of the radiator. In spite of his dad's impatience with him, Reese had picked up a lot of information from the man. And for that, he was grateful. Which surprised him. He'd never felt gratitude toward his father. Never felt anything but anger, hurt and disdain. But now he had something to hold on to. Something good about his dad.

"Well, thanks again. You come on over to the house anytime. We're so proud of how you've changed," Harry said.

"Yes, stop in for dinner next time. I'll make a chocolate cake for you," Caroline said.

Reese smiled and nodded, but he couldn't speak. A lump had formed in his throat. Several people in the restaurant were looking his way. He didn't want this attention. And suddenly, having dinner with Katie and Chrissy didn't seem like such a good idea.

Megan Marshall, the owner of the restaurant, stood beside the cash register. A glint of recognition flashed in her eyes.

"Why don't you sit over there?" She spoke low and smiled as she slid the till drawer closed. She pointed toward a booth tucked back in a corner, where Reese could remain more anonymous.

The woman seemed to know that he didn't want to engage in conversation with other people. Mrs. Watkins had told him that Megan was married to Jared Marshall, the fire management officer. They'd been married only a short time. Apparently Megan had lost her first husband fighting a wildfire a couple years earlier. Since she was afraid of losing another husband to a fire, it had taken her a long time to agree to marry the FMO. No doubt she understood how Reese was feeling right now, and her kindness touched his heart.

Smiling his thanks, he headed that way with Chrissy and Katie in tow. Megan handed him a newspaper as he passed.

"If you see someone you don't want to talk to, just hold the paper up to hide your face." She spoke quietly, but it was obvious from Katie's expression that she overheard.

He nodded and slid into the booth, grateful for Megan's protection. Chrissy sat beside him, with Katie on the other side of the table, no more than an arm's reach away. He thought about raking leaves with them a short time earlier and how he'd almost kissed Katie. For a few moments, he'd forgotten who she was and who he was, and all that stood between them.

Megan brought menus, and crayons for Chrissy. They ordered soft drinks and the waitress disappeared.

"What was that all about?" Katie asked.

He glanced at her. "What do you mean?"

"When did you work on Harry Carter's truck?"

"Yesterday," he said.

"I understand, but how did it come about?"

He shrugged. "They were broken down on the side of the road. I couldn't just leave them stranded there, so I stopped to help. Once we got his truck back home, I worked on it, to make it run better."

Her mouth dropped open and she stared at him from across the table.

"It was no big deal, Katie," he said.

She blinked. "No big deal? I'm stunned that you would do all of that."

He shrugged. "I thought it was time to make amends. When I offered to help, they didn't recognize me at first."

He didn't tell her about the cool reception he'd received from the Carters once they knew who he was. Thankfully, they warmed up to him after he'd apologized. It had felt good to make restitution by fixing their truck.

Megan set glasses of iced drinks in front of them.

"Something cold to sip on while you wait for your food," she said, sliding her hands into the front pocket of her apron. "And just so you're aware, there are several hotshots on the other side of the restaurant. My husband,

Jared, is having pie with Sean and Tessa Nash, and Harlie Harland. They're all members of the crew."

Reese went very still. Under normal circumstances, he would have sought them out to talk. After all, Sean had come to the motel to offer him a job. But right now, he still didn't want to speak to anyone involved with the media or the firefighting profession.

"I can tell them to leave you alone, if you like," Megan offered.

No, he didn't want to be rude. "That's okay. Thanks anyway."

"Sure. Whatever you need, don't be afraid to ask. Firefighters stick together." She whirled away, moving behind the counter to reach for the coffeepot.

His gaze followed her as she made the rounds, filling cups at each table. He appreciated her kindness, but maybe it had been a mistake to come here.

The bell over the door tinkled. His hands trembling, Reese lifted the newspaper, feeling like a coward. He'd never been like this before. Usually, he was outgoing.

He scanned the columns of the paper, including a fun article Katie had written about the renovation of an old stagecoach station just outside town. Hmm. She was a good writer, but he wasn't surprised. From what he knew about her, she was good at everything.

"Great article in the newspaper today." He showed her the paper and smiled.

"Did Mommy write that?" Chrissy pointed at the picture.

"She sure did, and she did a good job," Reese said.

"Wow, Mom. Everyone will read what you wrote. That's so cool." The girl's voice was filled with awe and respect.

"Thank you." Katie smiled, looking pleased by their compliments.

"You still have your binoculars, I see." Reese touched the lanyard hanging around Chrissy's neck.

"Yes, Papa Charlie let me borrow them," she said.

"How would you like to go fishing with me tomorrow?" Reese asked.

"Fishing?" Chrissy crinkled her button nose.

Reese hesitated. "Yeah. Don't you like to fish?"

"Sure. I go with Papa and Mommy when we can get away from the motel, but I don't like to touch the worms." She scrunched her mouth in disgust and a shudder swept her slender shoulders.

Reese laughed. "How about if I hook the bait for you?"

"Fine. Can we go, Mom? Please?" The girl bounced gently on her seat.

"I'm not sure..." Uncertainty filled Katie's voice.

He met Katie's eyes and tried to smile. "The invitation includes you, too. I'll pick you up around seven o'clock, if that's all right."

She hiked her brows. "Wouldn't you rather we just drove up to the cabin?"

"No, I've got something I need to do in town early in the morning. I've put it off long enough. I can pick you up."

"What could you have to do in town so early on a Saturday morning?"

He hesitated. "It's personal."

Actually, he didn't want to tell her that he planned to visit his mother at the local cemetery.

"Okay, we'll be ready."

He was grateful that she didn't push for more information. A happy feeling of relief blanketed him. He couldn't deny that he was excited to be with them both.

"I'll get the fishing license on my way home today," he said.

"Get one for a bi-i-ig fish." Chrissy opened her arms wide to make her point.

He chuckled. "It's all the same, sweetheart. One license covers both the big and small fish."

"But you'll have to clean them, too." The girl grimaced.

"Don't worry. I'll take care of it for you." In a spontaneous gesture, he reached out and tickled Chrissy's ribs. The child squealed, but he could tell she liked the attention.

He inclined his head and smiled. He didn't mind cleaning the fish for his little girl. In fact, he was glad to do it. For some crazy reason, he felt protective toward both Katie and their daughter. And he realized that, except for his mother, he'd never felt this way before. Since he'd returned home, he was having a lot of firsts. Things inside of him were changing, shifting, rearranging. Almost as if he were mentally making room in his life for others. An odd notion, but he couldn't explain it to himself.

Out of the corner of his eye, he saw Sean Nash and the other hotshots walk over to the cash register. They looked his way, saw him, and one of the men took a step toward him.

No! Reese didn't want to speak to them. Not now. He knew that they'd offer condolences and possibly ask him questions about the fire. Questions he didn't want to answer. And suddenly, the happiness he'd felt moments earlier evaporated like a puff of smoke. The room closed in on him. A blaze of panic prickled his skin. He had to get out of here. Right now.

"Reese, are you all right?" Katie asked from the other side of the table.

She was looking at him, the corners of her eyes creased with confusion. His expression must have given him away. He was vaguely aware of her taking Chrissy's hand and drawing the child to her feet. "Come here, honey."

"Hi, Reese." Sean Nash smiled. "Can I introduce you to my wife, Tessa?"

The woman smiled, flipping her long golden-brown hair back over her shoulder. She was dressed identical to her husband in spruce-green pants and a blue T-shirt with the Minoa Hotshot logo on it. Jared wore his drab olive-green Forest Service shirt, a bronze shield pinned to his front pocket.

"Hi, Reese. It's nice to meet you," Tessa said.

"And this is Jared Marshall, our FMO." Sean continued with the introductions. "And Harlie Harland, one of our squad leaders."

"Hi, man." Harlie stuck out his hand and smiled widely. "I understand you're thinking about working for our crew. We'd be glad to have you. We need experienced firefighters like you."

Reese stood slowly and shook the man's hand. He locked his knees to keep them from trembling.

"Hello." He got the word out, unable to say anything more.

"I was sorry to hear about your crew. If there's anything we can do, or if you just need to talk, we've got your back." Harlie winked at him.

"Thanks," Reese murmured. The man's words seemed genuine, but Reese had no desire to talk with anyone about his problems.

"With your experience, you'd fit in perfectly with the crew. I hope you'll consider the offer," Jared Marshall said.

He hadn't discussed it with Katie yet, but he wanted to help with Chrissy's financial support. He certainly didn't want to be a deadbeat dad. He had to think about the future. His daughter would undoubtedly need things like braces and a college fund. He couldn't help with that if he didn't have a job.

Katie touched his arm, speaking in a low tone. "Reese, do we need to leave?"

"No, I'm fine." But he wasn't. His mind buzzed with the memory of the fire and the screams of men. It came upon him so fast that he didn't understand it. His doctor had said he might experience some symptoms of PTSD, but he'd laughed it off. Now he realized it was still a problem.

Katie faced the firefighters, speaking in a pleasant tone. "I'm sorry to break this up, folks, but we were just leaving."

Reese jerked his head toward her, confused for a moment. When she reached out and rested a hand on his arm, he flinched. Her touch was warm and gentle, soothing the fog of panic in his brain.

"We won't keep you, but do think about that job. You know where to find me," Sean said, his voice congenial and sincere.

The firefighters moved away and Reese drew a deep inhalation. He was finally able to breathe again. To think clearly.

"I had your dinner prepared to go. I can see you need to get out of here." Megan handed him a plastic bag with to-go containers inside. Barely understanding what he was doing, he held the handle tightly wrapped around his fingers.

Reese fumbled for his wallet, dropped it on the floor and waited while Chrissy retrieved it for him.

"Here you go," the girl said.

"Thanks." He gave her a feeble smile.

Megan pushed them toward the door. "You can settle up with me the next time you come in."

Again, he was grateful. Both Megan and Katie seemed to know that he was desperate to get out of here.

"Thanks, I will," he murmured.

"Come on," Katie said. And taking his arm, she steered him out of the restaurant and over to her car.

Chrissy trotted after them, her innocent face torn with worry. "What's wrong, Mommy? Why are we going so fast? I thought we were gonna eat in the restaurant."

"Something has come up. We're in a hurry now, sweetums. Everything will be fine," Katie said.

Hearing her soft voice and words of reassurance to their daughter eased Reese's tension, as well. He opened the door to her car and waited for them to slide inside, then joined them.

Katie sat in the driver's seat. Now that they were alone, Reese breathed deeply, feeling instant relief.

"Can you take me back to my truck?" he asked.

"Yes, but I want to make sure you're all right before we leave you," she said.

He snorted. "I'm fine. You don't need to babysit me."

Chrissy sat in her booster seat in back, her eyes wide with confusion. "Mommy, what's going on?"

"Nothing, dear. Everything's fine," Katie spoke in a calm voice.

Reese jerked when the child popped her seat belt and leaned forward to press her cheek against his shoulder. She wrapped one thin arm across his chest. "I'm sorry you don't feel well, Daddy. Is there anything I can do for you?"

His heart pinched hard. An overwhelming warmth suffused his entire being. He wondered how this little girl had crawled into his heart so quickly. He could hardly believe someone this wonderful belonged to him.

"I'm fine, sweetheart. I've got you. What more could I want?" he said.

She hugged him tighter in response. "And we've got Mommy, too."

"Yes, we've got Mommy, too," he conceded. He looked over at Katie. "You sure have done a good job with her. She's sweet and polite and well mannered."

Katie flushed red as a fire engine, looking embarrassed yet pleased by his praise. "Thank you, but she seems to come by it naturally. She's been an easy child to raise thus far." Then she chuckled. "I hope she's this wonderful when she's a teenager."

He laughed in turn. "I have no doubt she'll still be wonderful, because she's ours."

Katie blinked at that, then looked away. Maybe this was all wrong. And yet it felt so right, sitting here in the car with the two of them, being a part of their life. But Katie had made her feelings clear. She didn't want him. He'd been forced upon her because he was Chrissy's father. And that was that.

He reached up and squeezed Chrissy's arm. "I'll be okay, sweetheart. You don't need to worry about me."

"Have you seen a doctor for your PTSD?" Katie asked.

He didn't meet her eyes, conscious of Chrissy listening in. "How did you know I have PTSD?"

Katie shrugged. "I pay attention. Remember, I used to want to be a doctor."

"Yeah, I remember. And yes, I've seen someone. The attacks are happening less often, but they still come on unexpectedly. I've never had a big reaction like this before and I'm sorry if I upset you and Chrissy."

He didn't know why he was confiding this information

to her. It just seemed to come out. But he didn't understand what was wrong with him and he hated showing any weakness.

"What do you think set it off this time?" Katie asked.

He released a deep sigh. "I think I felt a bit cornered by the hotshots. I know they mean well, but I feared they might ask questions about the fire. But they didn't, so I'm hoping I'm more at ease with them in the future."

"It's only been a matter of weeks. I think it's normal for you to feel the way you do. Give yourself some time. But the power of prayer can help, too," Katie said.

Time. Yes, maybe time would help. But prayer? He was still skeptical. And yet her deep, abiding faith touched his heart. He'd been living without anyone's help for so long. But now he realized he needed more than himself to make it through this current difficulty. Maybe it was time for him to build a relationship with God. He just wasn't sure he had enough faith to do that.

"Are you all right, Daddy?" Chrissy asked again.

"Yes, I'm fine, bug." He purposefully used Charlie's nickname for her, hoping to put her at ease.

The girl smiled. "Are we still going fishing tomorrow?"

Reese chuckled and reached back to run his hand over one of her long ponytails. "Of course we are. And bring your compass. I'll give you another lesson on how to use it."

"Oh, goodie!" Chrissy said.

"Are you sure you're up to it?" Katie asked, her hand resting on the door latch.

He nodded. "Of course. Fishing is a relaxing pastime."

"And you're sure that you're okay now?" She was looking at him with those soft brown eyes, as though searching inside him for the truth.

"Yes. I appreciate your concern, but you don't need to worry about me."

They talked for a few more minutes, with Katie's piercing gaze studying his face for signs of duress. Finally, she seemed satisfied that he was all right and drove him back to Mrs. Watkins's place, where he got into the truck Charlie had loaned him. As mother and daughter pulled away to go home, Reese returned Chrissy's wave.

He started up his vehicle but didn't put it in gear. Instead, he sat there and idled the engine. He couldn't believe the kindness of the Minoa Hotshots. Instead of recriminations, they'd surrounded him with support. And Katie. He knew she resented him for abandoning her. Yet she'd stayed with him when she thought he was in trouble. And Chrissy with her gentle hug of encouragement… Their kindness startled him. It had been a very long time since someone cared about him, and an even longer time since he'd cared about someone besides himself.

Chapter Nine

This was a mistake. Katie felt it in her bones. She never should have agreed to this fishing trip. Because the more time she spent with the man, the more she liked him. And that would only lead to more pain when he finally left town.

"How come we had to get up so early?" Chrissy grumbled as she rubbed her eyes.

Morning sunlight streamed from the azure sky, and a mild breeze blew from the east. Dressed in shorts and a sweatshirt, the girl stood in the back alleyway and hugged her stuffed teddy bear close. Katie wasn't thrilled by the early time, either. It was her one morning to sleep in.

Reese loaded their things into the back of his truck. He'd stopped at the motel to pick them up promptly at seven o'clock. In spite of the hour, he was freshly shaven, looking lean and strong in his faded blue jeans, boots and T-shirt. His dark hair had just a hint of gel in it, parted down the right side and slicked back. He looked good. Too good.

Katie averted her eyes.

"Early morning is when the fish bite the most," Reese said.

He laid a couple of lawn chairs in the back, then took

the picnic basket and first aid kit from Katie's hands. She caught his scent, a subtle mixture of spicy cologne and oranges.

Yesterday in the restaurant, he'd looked pale and startled. Like he was lost and didn't know how to act anymore. Katie wasn't sure how bad his PTSD was. She figured he needed a friend to talk to, but she didn't want it to be her.

He glanced at her oversize bag and gave her a lopsided smile that shot darts of charm straight to her heart. "What have you got in there, the kitchen sink?"

She laughed and adjusted the straps of the heavy bag. "No, just some extra towels, in case Chrissy wants to go swimming. I also brought you the morning newspaper, but you may not like what you see. There's a picture of you inside."

His eyebrows quirked. While she rummaged around in her bag for the paper, he stood nearby, wearing a deep frown.

"What picture?" he asked.

She unfolded the paper and held it up for his view. He took it and scanned the article. The front page showed a picture of him standing in Mrs. Watkins's yard with the headline Local Hero Mends Fences.

He jerked his head up and stared at Katie. "Did you take this snapshot?"

Katie heard the accusation in his voice and shook her head. "No, I did not."

"Then who did?"

She pointed at the small print, which listed the photo credit. "Bruce Miller. When Chrissy and I saw you at Mrs. Watkins's house yesterday, I noticed a blue sedan parked down the block. Someone was inside, smoking.

The man looked vaguely familiar, but I wasn't sure. Then when I saw the article today, I knew it was him."

Reese's eyes narrowed on the article and he shook his head in disgust. "Bruce Miller."

"Do you know him?" she asked.

"Yeah, he's an independent journalist that writes award-winning articles for the National News Registry," Reese said. "He was here at the motel that first day when I got into town. He won't seem to take no for an answer. Now it appears that he's going around town interviewing anyone willing to talk, so he can get a story on me."

"I'm sorry, Reese." She hated that he might believe she had any part in this. She'd been writing about him, too, but didn't plan to publish her story unless he gave his permission. She'd seen firsthand how tortured he was over losing his hotshot crew. She planned to wait until he seemed more at ease before asking him if she could let her editor publish it.

"My work at Mrs. Watkins's house was personal," Reese said. "I didn't want to draw attention to it. Most of the media has left town, but it seems that some reporters are still hanging around."

"I know. And I'm sorry, Reese. Truly I am," she said.

And she meant every word. Maybe her article would never be printed, but that didn't matter if he was hurting.

Reese reached for Chrissy's bag and he gave his daughter a teasing frown. "What is all this stuff?"

"My things. I need them," she said.

Katie almost laughed out loud. Chrissy had packed her dolly and blanket, a jacket, several books and a few other nonsensical "necessities." A complete girlie girl.

"It looks like you're packing for a month-long trip," Reese teased, but he stashed her stuff in the back like a good daddy.

"I'm bringing my compass with me, too." Chrissy reached into her pocket and pulled out the case for his inspection.

"Good! I'm sure we'll have time for another orienteering lesson."

"Orienteering?" she asked in a quizzical tone.

"Yes, it's the skill of being able to navigate your way by using a map and compass in an unfamiliar area." He leaned down and welcomed the girl's tight hug, brushing a curl of hair back from her cheek as he smiled into her eyes.

Seeing this man interact with her daughter in such a personal way tweaked Katie's heart. For just a moment, she wished they could always be like this. That they could be a real family. But thinking like that would get her nothing but trouble. Reese wasn't interested in a family. He never had been. She should enjoy the day and take it at face value. It was a fishing trip, nothing more.

Charlie came outside, packing a digital camera. "Picture time."

"Yes, let's get a picture of Reese and Chrissy together," Katie said.

Reese willingly hunkered down and pulled Chrissy onto his knee. They both smiled widely as Charlie clicked the camera.

"Now let's get one of all of you together," Charlie said.

Katie stepped back, feeling off balance. "Dad..."

"Yeah, Mom. Get in here with us," Chrissy urged.

Before she knew what was happening, Katie found herself standing next to Reese, with Chrissy in front of them.

"Say cheese," Charlie urged.

Katie tried to smile but feared it would look more like

a grimace. Her dad snapped the picture and she breathed a sigh of relief that it was over.

Charlie hugged Chrissy, tickling her ribs. "You have fun today, all right, bug?"

"Papa! Stop that." The girl squealed, but it was obvious she was enjoying herself.

Charlie laughed and finally released her, then turned to embrace his daughter. Leaning close, Katie accepted his kiss on her cheek, then tensed when he whispered in her ear. "Relax, Mom. Our little girl is gonna be just fine with her dad. Go and have fun."

Katie snapped her head around to look at Reese, fearing he might have overheard. Thankfully, he was buckling Chrissy into her booster seat and didn't appear to have noticed.

"How many fish do you think we'll catch today?" Chrissy asked, when they were all settled and on their way.

Reese waved at Charlie as he pulled out of the alley and onto the dirt road leading up to Cove Mountain. "I don't know. It's a calm day, so we should be able to catch enough for dinner."

Chrissy glanced at her mom. "Are you gonna invite Daddy to supper?"

Oh, no. Now that Chrissy had said it out loud, Katie didn't see a way to avoid an invitation. After all, when they went fishing, they usually ate their catch for their evening meal. Except Chrissy, who always wanted macaroni and cheese.

Before Katie could respond, Chrissy whirled toward Reese. "You're coming to supper with us, aren't you?"

"Um, that's up to your mother, sweetheart." Reese stared straight ahead.

The girl swung around to face her mother, her nose

crinkled in a perturbed frown. "He can come, can't he, Mom?"

"Sure," Katie said, without much enthusiasm. "You'll have to drive us back home, anyway. You might as well stay for supper."

"Thanks. That sounds nice," he said.

They soon arrived at Cove Lake and Reese killed the engine. They all climbed out and he unloaded their things, including a tackle box, which Katie recognized as her father's. It was filled with colorful lures, sinkers, hooks and extra fishing line. He looped the strap over his shoulder, then hefted the two fishing poles.

"Are you ready to go?" he asked, looking first at Katie, then at Chrissy.

"I am!" the child responded.

"Then let's go fishing." He headed toward the lake. Chrissy was right beside him, skipping over rocks, plants and fallen logs.

Katie followed, grateful that Reese didn't seem to be overly bothered by the newspaper article and the invasion of his privacy. As she walked, she listened to Chrissy's buoyant chatter and the deep timbre of Reese's laughter. She inhaled the fresh air and gave a quick shudder.

Being together in the mountains like this did something to her. It set off a longing she had suppressed since she'd had Chrissy. And having Reese here only made that longing worse.

Reese didn't know what to think. Had Katie taken his picture when he'd been working over at Mrs. Watkins's house? After all, she was a reporter for the *Minoa Daily News*. A big story might advance her career. Especially if it got picked up by the national news.

Surely she wouldn't stoop that low. Bruce Miller's

name was captioned in the article. Katie hadn't known about it. He could trust her. Couldn't he?

At the lake, she sat on a large boulder next to him, holding Chrissy's fishing pole. When Chrissy caught her first fish, she'd cried and begged Reese to throw it back. Not knowing how to handle her tears, he'd done as she asked, wondering what they would eat for supper without any fish in their basket. When she got the fishing line caught in her hair, he'd patiently untangled it. She'd lost interest in the activity after that. Now she strolled along the pebbled beach, picking up colorful rocks.

"She never keeps the fish she catches. She's too tenderhearted," Katie said.

"Tenderhearted is good for a girl her age. I just wish she was having more fun," Reese said.

"She is, believe me."

He glanced doubtfully at his daughter. She was bent over, picking up a glistening rock. Her teddy bear hung limp from her left hand. "How can you tell?"

Katie pointed at the child. "Look how she's playing on the beach. And listen. What do you hear?"

Reese paused, holding his fishing pole with both hands. The girl's lilting voice rose through the air in a sweet song he'd learned at church as a child. He couldn't remember the words but knew the melody well enough.

"She's singing," he said.

Katie nodded. "Yes. Which means she's happy. Besides, she'd let us know if she wasn't having fun. Believe me."

"But she cried when she caught a fish," he said.

Katie shrugged as she leaned the fishing rod against an outcropping of rock. "That's just a girl for you, Reese. She's having fun. Trust me."

"But she's making such a racket that she'll probably

scare all the fish away." He chuckled, wondering if he'd ever figure out how the opposite gender worked. Being a father was so new to him, yet he couldn't deny that he liked it so far. But he hated it when girls cried.

"Don't worry. If we don't catch any fish, I've got some T-bone steaks in the fridge. Dad can fire up the barbecue while I make a salad and slice some watermelon," Katie said.

"That sounds delicious." In fact, he couldn't remember ever having a barbecue with his parents. But he'd cooked a lot of steaks with his hotshot buddies. And the fun memories brought a dull ache to his heart.

"Did you visit your parents at the cemetery this morning?" Katie asked.

"I visited my mom." Gazing at the sparkling lake, he tugged on his fishing line, slowly reeling it in. He'd neglected his mother when she'd been alive and he regretted it more than he could say. This morning, he'd told her how sorry he was. He just wished she was still here and he could wrap his arms around her and be a better son. In fact, he'd made a promise to her that morning. That he'd change. That he'd be the kind of man she had raised him to be. The kind of man she could be proud of.

"What about your dad?" Katie asked.

He quirked his mouth. "As far as I'm concerned, my father can lie in his casket and rot."

Katie flinched. "That's rather harsh."

He turned away, hating to let her see this dark side of him. His mom had raised him to be a Christian. To love and serve the Lord. To be a good, hardworking, honorable man. And though Reese had gone to church when he was a child, by the time he became a teenager, he'd wanted nothing to do with God. He didn't know if he could ever forgive his father for the hurt he'd caused them, and he didn't want to involve God in his feelings of anger and isolation.

"My father wasn't a nice man, Katie. You already know that, so let's not pretend. Because of him, life was beyond difficult growing up in my parents' home," he said.

She shifted her weight beside him and he turned his head. Her beautiful brown eyes were tinged with sadness. "I know your father was an alcoholic, but maybe it's time to forgive him. After all, he's gone now and it's in the past."

Reese snorted. "Forgive him? I left because of him. The night of our high school graduation, after I took you home from the dance, my father was in another drunken rage. He beat me so badly that he broke my nose, Katie."

"Oh, Reese. I'm so sorry." She covered her mouth with one hand, looking repulsed.

"I wasn't a kid anymore, Katie. I was eighteen years old and tall enough to look him in the eye. I knew if I didn't leave, I might kill him one day. I knew that was no good. That I was becoming someone I detested. So I got on a bus and left town early the next morning. As I told you before, I begged Mom to go with me, but she refused. She wouldn't leave my dad. She said she loved him. But I didn't. I hated him. And so I left. I called Mom about a year later, after I'd found a job and got settled with a place to live. But in all honesty, I wanted nothing to do with this town ever again."

"I'm sorry to hear that," Katie said.

Reese caught the throb of hurt in her voice.

"I did think about you often over the years, though," he said.

She lifted her eyebrows in disbelief. "Really?"

"Yes, it's true."

"Then why didn't you contact me?"

He shrugged, feeling ashamed of himself. "Honestly, I thought I didn't deserve a girl as good as you. I figured you must have gone to college, become a doctor and married some physicist or something. I figured you were happily living a life of luxury in a big city somewhere. You didn't want to be shackled to a guy like me."

She shook her head. "Is that what you really thought?"

He nodded. "You were great, Katie. Smart and hardworking. So talented. Good at everything you ever did. You deserved better than a boy like me from the wrong side of the tracks."

"Don't you think that was for me to decide?" she asked.

"I suppose so. I'm sorry now that I didn't ask." And he meant it. Every word. At the time, he'd been so filled with anger and hate. He didn't show it outwardly, but he'd had very little self-esteem. Had been too wounded to stop and think that maybe he had hurt Katie, too. That maybe she needed him as much as he needed her.

"We all have our problems to cope with. Even me," Katie said. "Maybe your dad had an even more rotten childhood than you did. Who knows what problems he was carrying around that made him bury himself in a bottle. Maybe if he'd gotten some help, he could have overcome his addiction. No matter what, you don't need to carry your hurt and anger anymore. You can hand it over to the Lord and let Him carry it for you."

Reese didn't respond. Instead, he changed the topic. But he couldn't help wondering about what Katie had said. She made forgiveness sound so easy. Like all he had to do was tell God all of his sorrows, that he regretted his mistakes, and he could move on and let it go. But he'd been angry for so long. How could he just hand it over to the Lord? He wasn't sure, but he sensed it would require a lot of prayer. He'd have to actively seek out God. To ask forgiveness and resolve to become a better man. In spite of Katie's convictions, Reese wasn't sure he could do that. Not right now when he was hurting so much. Maybe never.

Chapter Ten

Katie sat on a pew in the redbrick church house and folded her hands in her lap. Chrissy was sandwiched between her and Charlie, waiting for the Sunday service to start. Soft organ music filtered through the air, a hymn that set the reverent tone for the meeting. But Katie couldn't help feeling restless.

Her discussion with Reese the day before still troubled her. Until he had talked about the horrible fight with his father that caused him to leave town, Katie hadn't realized how difficult life must have been for him. His dad had broken his nose, and Reese had feared he might kill him one day. She'd encouraged him to forgive his father, yet she felt like a hypocrite. In her heart of hearts, she knew it wasn't fair to ask Reese to forgive his dad when she hadn't yet forgiven him. Now she knew that his leaving town had nothing to do with her. Nothing at all. Maybe she had judged him unfairly. Maybe…

"Daddy!"

Katie turned. Planting her knees on the bench, Chrissy faced the back of the building and waved.

A stutter of silence swept over the room. Even the music stopped on a discordant note. Megan and Jared

Marshall, and numerous other people in the congregation, turned to look. Their eyes widened, their mouths dropped open. And Katie didn't need to ask why.

Reese stood in the double doorway, the morning sunlight silhouetting his tall figure. No doubt everyone was surprised to see him walk through the church doors, but that wasn't what had given them such a shock. They'd overheard Chrissy. She'd called him Daddy and they were now putting two and two together.

Katie swallowed a groan as she lowered her head and stared at the tips of her strappy high heels. A flush of heat washed over her, prickling her skin with mortification. How she wished she could disappear. Word would soon be all over town that Reese Hartnett was little Chrissy Ashmore's father. Everyone would know. Katie would be the brunt of gossip once more and there was nothing she could do to stop it.

Chrissy shifted restlessly, her face drawn with excitement. Katie reached up to quiet her, her peripheral vision catching Reese's movements. Without a word, he quickly took a seat in the back pew, close to the doors. All alone.

With his hair slicked back, he was dressed in a pair of navy slacks, a beautiful blue paisley tie and a white oxford shirt that fit him to perfection. Probably his best clothes. Katie wondered mildly if he owned a dress suit, but it wouldn't have mattered. Even without looking closely, she could see that he was freshly shaven. More handsome than a man had a right to be.

Seeing him sitting by himself, Katie felt her heart give a powerful squeeze. She naturally homed in on him like a heat-seeking missile and couldn't help wondering why. She told herself it was because he was Chrissy's dad. It surely had nothing to do with his rustic good looks. Or did it?

When Chrissy waved at him, he gave Katie an uncertain smile and winked. At least he hadn't winced when he'd heard his daughter call out to him. Katie realized how much courage it must have taken for him to come here today. A powerful surge of compassion swept over her when she contemplated how hard he was trying to be a better man. Going around town to perform good deeds and right the wrongs he'd done as a youth. Coming here to church when he wasn't sure he'd be welcomed.

Charlie swiveled in his seat, saw Reese sitting there and immediately stood. Without a word, he clasped his cane in one hand and Chrissy's hand in the other and led her to the back pew, where they joined Reese. Numerous people watched this scene, leaning their heads close as they whispered together.

This time, Katie couldn't contain her groan. Great! Just great. Having raised her daughter out of wedlock, she thought she'd become immune to the gossip. Where Reese was concerned, she was wrong. Now her family was sitting in the back pew. Without her. She was the one who was all alone. No matter what he'd done to her, unintentionally or otherwise, Katie couldn't abandon Reese. She was ashamed that it had been her father who first stepped forward to do the right thing and welcome him to church.

Standing, she hurried to the back to join her family. She almost bit her tongue when Charlie saw her coming and quickly reached over and pulled Chrissy in to sit between him and Reese. Since her father sat against the end of the pew, Katie had no choice but to sit next to Reese.

"What are you doing here?" she whispered as she settled beside him.

"Honestly, I was wondering the same thing."

His boyish grin and sparkling eyes did something

to her insides. No matter what promises she'd made to herself about not becoming attached to him again, she couldn't help wanting to comfort him. Especially after the things he'd told her the day before.

"Don't look so shocked, Katie. The building isn't going to fall in on top of us." He glanced up at the ceiling. "At least, I don't think it will."

"I...I'm glad you're here. There's nothing wrong with worshipping God. In fact, I think most of the problems in the world would be cured if people would include God in their lives," she said.

He lifted one shoulder. "I figured it was time."

"It's good to see you here." Charlie reached behind Chrissy and patted Reese's shoulder.

To make matters worse, Chrissy snuggled against her daddy's side, as if she belonged there. And Katie figured she did. But people were watching. There would be no way to keep this quiet now.

Reese lifted an arm and wrapped it around Chrissy just as the meeting began. And suddenly, Katie saw him with different eyes. No longer was he a belligerent, rebellious teenager. Now he was Chrissy's daddy. A man who the little girl freely loved and trusted.

Looking up, Katie saw several people gaping at them in open curiosity. She could see the questions in their eyes. The wonderment as they tried to figure out her relationship with the man. And something hardened inside her. No matter what they thought, it was none of their business. Katie had to live her life. She had to do what was right for her daughter.

Locking her jaw, Katie stared right back, until their faces flushed red with embarrassment and they turned frontward. They sang a hymn and later listened to a sermon from the Gospels on feeding the five thousand with a few loaves of bread and two small fishes.

As Katie contemplated the message, she glanced at Reese and saw that he also listened intently. Out of small things, great things were accomplished. Out of faith, miracles occurred.

She was so grateful that Reese had come this far. That he was interested in being a father to their daughter. That they could be friends. But she doubted they could ever be anything more. Reese would move on with his life and possibly find someone else to love and marry. He might even have more children one day, and that thought left Katie feeling sad and empty inside.

The meeting soon ended and Reese, Katie and her family congregated in the outer foyer with numerous other people. Reese edged toward the door, as if eager to escape. Maybe he'd had enough. But Chrissy cut him off.

"You're coming to Sunday dinner, aren't you?" she asked.

"Of course he is," Charlie said.

Reese glanced at Katie, his eyes filled with doubt. "Is that okay?"

She scoffed. "Yes, you're always welcome in our home."

But something held her back. A fear she couldn't explain. As though she were facing a heartache she wouldn't be able to bear. And the more time she spent with this man, the closer they became, the more intense the feeling.

"My daddy's a hero."

Katie jerked around and saw Chrissy talking to Caleb and June Marshall. The two kids were a bit older, but they were friends and often had playdates together.

"I think anyone who survives a wildfire is a hero," June said.

"Yeah, our dad is a hero, too. He saved us from a fire last year," Caleb said.

Megan and Jared Marshall stood nearby, smiling and listening to every word. They didn't comment, but Katie saw their knowing gazes shift between her and Reese. Well, no sense in hiding the truth. Katie met their eyes, keeping her composure.

Jared stepped forward and offered Reese his hand. "I'm glad you could make it today."

"It's good to be here," Reese said.

Katie listened with ambivalence. Yes, she was glad Reese was here, but she had no idea what it really meant. Nor did it change anything for her and Chrissy. Once Reese left town, their lives would continue like before. Maybe he'd return now and then for a brief visit. And that was good. Chrissy needed to see him. It was all that Katie dared ask for. Wasn't it? Right now, she wouldn't hope for anything more.

"Hey, Reese. It's good to see you." Sean Nash clapped him on the back.

Turning, Reese saw the man standing with his wife. Reese had met Tessa that day in the restaurant when they'd all crowded around him. He'd had a major panic attack. Now he waited for his PTSD to strike again, but it didn't. He felt uneasy with the numerous people looking at him, putting it all together that he was Chrissy's daddy. But no one was looking at him with censure or disapproval. They just smiled. And for some reason, he didn't want to run away. Not this time. In fact, he felt their camaraderie. Their genuine friendship.

"It's good to be here," he said, liking this new feeling.

He glanced at Katie and saw a flash of doubt in her eyes, but she smiled. She was holding up well, considering their daughter had announced openly to everyone that he was her dad. Maybe he shouldn't have come here. A sinner like him might not be acceptable to the Lord. And that was when an idea occurred to him. Maybe God hadn't abandoned him, after all. Maybe it was he who had abandoned the Lord.

"Do you know what this young man did?" Mrs. Watkins came out of nowhere, pushing her walker in front of her. Her elderly voice vibrated with happiness as she spoke to the group. "He cleaned up my entire yard and mended my fence, too."

"I saw the story in the newspaper. Our town needs more positive news like that," Megan said.

Reese blinked in response. He hadn't intended for anyone to find out.

"He brought me two cords of wood for the winter and chopped and stacked it all into a neat pile," Mr. Coleman said.

Charlie smiled widely. "He reroofed my shed."

Reese shifted his weight, a nervous flush of embarrassment heating his face. "It was my pleasure."

He longed to flee, but there'd be no quick escape now. Not with Mrs. Watkins clinging to his arm and several other people blocking his path to the door.

"Have you got somewhere to go for Sunday dinner?" Tessa asked. "I've got a roast in the slow cooker at home and you're more than welcome to join us."

"Oh, no." Mrs. Watkins frowned. "Why don't you come over to my house? I've got a nice chicken I'm frying."

Reese glanced at Katie. She stood beside her father, her face pale. No doubt this day was rather difficult for her, and he couldn't help wondering how she was taking all this in. When he'd come here, he'd had no idea that

Chrissy might blurt out that he was her father. He hated causing Katie any more difficulties.

"I'm sorry, but I've already got an invitation for Sunday dinner. But thank you. Maybe another time," he said.

Frankly, there was nowhere he'd rather be than with Katie, Chrissy and Charlie. But he was surprised when a brief look of relief flashed in Katie's eyes. Or had he imagined it? Surely she didn't care if he came to supper. Did she?

"Let me see, you two graduated from high school together, didn't you?" Mrs. Marley asked Katie.

"Um, yes, we did." Katie's voice sounded even enough, but her smile didn't quite reach her eyes.

"And Reese is Chrissy's father?" Mrs. Marley persisted, her eyes narrowed like a hawk's.

Katie turned aside and waved to her daughter, ignoring the question. "Come on, Chrissy. We've got to get home."

She started edging her way toward the door, and Reese couldn't blame her. He hoped that, now people knew he was Chrissy's dad, they would just accept it and move on. He couldn't help feeling compassion for Katie. During all the long, lonely years when she'd been the brunt of the town gossip and had to bite her tongue, he hadn't been here to comfort her. To offer her support and reassurance. But he was here now.

He faced Mrs. Marley and squared his shoulders. "Yes, I'm Chrissy's father."

The woman blinked in surprise. "Oh! So it is true."

"Yes."

Turning, he took Chrissy's hand and led her outside into the summer sunshine. Katie and Charlie followed. And when they stood in the parking lot, Charlie helped the little girl into her booster seat while Reese opened Katie's door for her.

"You didn't need to be rude," she said.

"I'm sorry, but I'm not very good at suffering fools."

She didn't look at him. From her locked jaw, Reese could tell she wasn't happy about today. He felt the urge to say something soothing. Something to let her know she didn't need to suffer this on her own any longer.

"Katie, I'm sorry about how it happened," he said. "But at least the news is out there now. No more hiding. You don't have to pretend anymore."

She slid into her seat, careful to keep her flowered dress from hiking up and showing too much leg. And he couldn't help thinking what a beautiful, modest woman she was. A woman much like his mother.

"Yes, everyone will know the truth. And after you leave town, I'll be left here to deal with the whispers behind my back." Reaching out, she pulled the door closed, effectively cutting off his reply.

"See you over at the house," Charlie called.

The man gave Reese a half smile, but it didn't help much. Right now, Reese was feeling like a heel. He nodded, wondering if he was still welcome to dinner. But deep inside, he knew he had to show up. No more running away. No more cowardice, no more hiding. It was time to put his past behind him. If he ever hoped to build any kind of future for himself and receive the healing power of God's redeeming love, he had to make a drastic change. And while he'd taken the first step by seeking the Lord, he now realized he needed to exercise some knee-mail and pray. Although that sounded simple, it wasn't. Not for him. In many ways, prayer was the most frightening thing Reese had contemplated facing since he'd returned to town.

Chapter Eleven

Katie leaned forward and set her half-empty glass of lemonade on the coffee table in the living room. Looking up, she glanced at Reese. He'd rested his head back against the recliner and closed his eyes. Chrissy lay cuddled at his side, clutching her teddy bear to her chest. Her eyes were shut, her fringe of lashes long and thick against her pale cheeks. She breathed deeply, telling Katie that she was asleep.

After Sunday dinner, they had washed the dishes as a family, then retired to watch some TV. Church had been rather exhausting for all of them. When Chrissy had announced that Reese was her daddy, Katie had been ready to run for the door. But now she reconsidered. She had to accept it. For good or bad, the news was out there. She had to take care of Chrissy. People could think what they liked. She had no control over anyone but herself. Besides, she'd never liked keeping secrets and now she didn't have any. Except for one. And she wouldn't share that with anyone, nor allow herself to dwell on it, either, because it would only lead to more heartache.

Reese shifted in the chair and brushed his hand over

Chrissy's arm, a careless, gentle caress. Maybe he wasn't asleep, after all, but just dozing.

A powerful surge rushed through Katie. A protective impulse to keep both Reese and her daughter safe and happy.

Charlie lay sprawled across the sofa, his soft snores stuttering in the air, along with the whoosh from the swamp cooler. The staccato voice of the evening news reporter made Katie wonder how any of them could sleep with all the racket. But the serene atmosphere was calming, the white noise soothing.

Stifling a yawn, she glanced at the clock hanging on the wall. Almost eight o'clock in the evening. The summer sun still glowed through the window, but Reese should get going if he didn't want to drive up the mountain in the dark. She was reluctant to disturb him. The serenity felt good. And she knew this was what she'd always wanted. A family of her own. What she would never dare hope for.

Reese opened his eyes and looked straight at her. She flinched, embarrassed to be caught staring. He gave her a lazy smile that caused an encompassing warmth to fill her heart. She couldn't describe how seeing him here in her home, holding their daughter in his strong embrace, made her feel. He'd loosened the collar of his white Oxford shirt and removed his paisley tie. Open and casual. He blinked his eyes, a jagged thatch of hair falling over his high forehead.

"Are you okay?" he asked.

"Yes, of course." She picked up her knitting and started another row, her hands moving like lightning as she twined the delicate yarn through her fingers.

"What are you making?" he asked.

She paused. "A baby afghan for Helen Sanders. She's

due next month and a group of us are throwing a baby shower for her. You remember Helen, don't you?"

She waited for his nod, then started knitting again. Helen had been a year older than them. A cute girl he'd dated a couple times.

"My mom used to knit," he said.

"That's right. She made an afghan for Chrissy. I'll have to show it to you sometime." She glanced at him, noticing his faraway look.

"I find the click of your needles strangely comforting."

What an odd thing to say. But she liked it anyway.

"I've got a friend who works for a construction company in Reno. He says they're hiring and he thinks I could get a job there," Reese said.

She tightened her fingers around the knitting needles and missed a stitch. She'd known this day would come. That he'd leave town, and she'd be left to raise Chrissy on her own again. But what other option did he have? He couldn't fight wildfires anymore. She accepted that. And he couldn't live in the cabin on Cove Mountain indefinitely. He had to find gainful employment and that wasn't likely to happen in this sleepy town. He'd have to leave. Eventually. And that thought made her stare.

"I'd come home regularly on weekends for visits," he said.

Home. Funny how he'd used that word. He had no family here anymore, except their daughter. Yet he still considered this his home.

"That would be nice. I'm sure Chrissy will miss you," Katie said.

He shifted his weight in the chair. "I'll miss her, too."

"Maybe I can drive Chrissy to Reno to visit you once in a while," she said.

"That would be nice."

They were talking like two old married people making plans for their life. And they weren't. Two old married people, that was. Yet Katie could hardly stand the thought of him leaving town for good. And she didn't understand why.

She finished the next row of her knitting, then set it aside in a wicker basket and padded across the room in her bare feet. After church, she'd changed out of her frilly dress and high heels and now wore faded blue jeans and a simple shirt. He gazed at her feet.

"I like your pink nail polish," he said.

She felt the heat of a flush rise up over her cheeks. She stood beside him, gazing down at their daughter. The soft light of love filled her heart and a warm fullness enveloped her chest.

"She's really out of it," Katie said.

Reese chuckled. "Yes, definitely tuckered out."

"Sunday seems to do that to a person. We come home ravenous, and after we eat, we just want to relax."

"No doubt the Lord knew we needed a rest day. That's probably why one of the commandments is to keep the Sabbath day holy," he said.

She blinked, stunned that he knew about that. All these years, she'd thought of him as a heathen who knew nothing about God. But he had surprised her once more.

"Maybe you're right." She felt self-conscious with him sitting so close. She almost reached out and took his hand, but she resisted the urge. What was wrong with her? She was feeling sentimental and lonely tonight, which didn't make sense.

"Can you carry Chrissy into her room? It's her bedtime," Katie said.

"Sure." He lowered the footrest. It gave a soft click as he sat up slowly, cradling their daughter in his arms.

Katie led the way down the narrow hall and he stepped into Chrissy's room. Books were stacked neatly on a shelf, the twin bed covered with a bunch of stuffed toys. Katie swept them aside and pulled the covers back. Reese laid the girl's head against the pillow, then drew a blanket over her.

"Aren't we gonna have prayers first?" Chrissy said in a sleepy voice. She opened one eye, then the other.

"I thought you were asleep," Katie said.

"I was, but I can't go to bed without prayers," the child insisted.

"Okay, let's do it," Katie said.

Chrissy slid off the bed and knelt on the soft rug. Folding her arms, she leaned against the mattress and stared up at them expectantly. Her parents. The two people she should be able to trust most in the entire world.

Katie immediately knelt beside her daughter and Reese followed suit. She wondered if he knew how to pray.

"Can you help me, Dad?" Chrissy looked at him with wide, innocent eyes.

Katie tensed, holding her breath.

Reese blinked, as though trying to remember what to do. And then he began in a halting voice, pausing periodically so that Chrissy could repeat the words after him. A simple prayer, asking God to watch after Grandpa Charlie and Mommy. He quickly closed in Jesus's name.

"Wait!" Chrissy looked up at Reese, a small crinkle in her forehead.

He stared back and whispered reverently, "What?"

Chrissy didn't explain, just bowed her head again.

"And please bless Daddy, so that he can find a new job and stay here in Minoa with us forever. Amen."

Chrissy climbed into bed, seeming oblivious to her stunned parents. The girl had pulled her teddy bear close and settled against her fluffy pillow before Reese and Katie could recover.

Reese leaned down and kissed her forehead.

"I love you, Daddy." The girl yawned sleepily.

His mouth dropped open and he blinked quickly. Katie got the impression he was overcome by emotion.

"I love you, too, sweetheart." His voice sounded soft and thoughtful, like he really meant it. And that caused Katie's heart to squeeze hard.

A knock on the door caused them all to turn. Charlie stood in the doorway and looked at Reese.

"Sorry to interrupt, but you have a visitor," he said.

Reese tilted his head, looking cautious. "Who is it?"

"It's Jared Marshall, the fire management officer," Charlie said.

"I'll finish tucking Chrissy in. You go on and speak with him," Katie said.

Reese stepped over to the door. He glanced back at her, holding her gaze for several long moments. Katie wasn't sure, but she thought he wanted to say something more. Then he turned and followed Charlie down the hall. She wanted to call Reese back, to ask him not to leave Minoa. To stay here with her and Chrissy. But she couldn't. She wouldn't beg. Wouldn't put herself in a situation where her heart could be broken again. If Reese chose to stay here, it must be his decision.

"Hi, Jared. What's up?"

Katie heard Reese greet the FMO in the living room, and then Jared's deep reply. "Can we talk in private?"

"Sure," Reese said.

Katie considered listening in but didn't think that was right. Instead, she clicked off the light in Chrissy's room and pulled the door closed before she went to her own room. A part of her couldn't help hoping that Jared was here to talk Reese into staying in Minoa on a permanent basis.

Jared lounged on the sofa and Reese sat opposite him in a recliner. As he did so, he noticed he no longer felt nervous around the FMO. No rush of panic filled his chest, no sweaty palms, no urge to run. Knowing this man was a friend, Reese felt calm, but curious.

"What's up?" he asked.

Jared tugged at the collar of his shirt. Like Reese, the man was missing the tie he'd worn to church earlier. But as a member of the clergy who worked with the teenage boys in their congregation, Jared had likely been involved in a variety of meetings that afternoon. And Reese couldn't help wishing he'd had a leader like Jared around when he'd been a youth. Someone to rescue him from himself. And that made Reese want to help other teenage boys who might be in the same situation. As soon as he got settled somewhere permanently, he was going to follow up on the idea.

"I was just wondering if you'd like to join the Minoa Hotshot Crew in the Fourth of July parade on Wednesday," Jared said.

Reese's spine stiffened. "Thanks, but I better not. I'm trying to stay out of the public eye. I don't want to give the media any more stories to write about."

Jared leaned forward and whispered in a conspiratorial tone. "What if you can go incognito?"

"Incognito?" Reese repeated.

"Yeah. I can promise that you'll have a great time, get to ride in the parade, and no one but us hotshots will have any idea it's you."

Reese smiled, his interest piqued. "Okay, I'll admit you've tantalized my curiosity. What exactly did you have in mind?"

Chapter Twelve

"Why didn't Daddy come to the parade with us?" Chrissy asked for the umpteenth time that morning.

Lifting two adult-sized folding chairs out of the back of the truck her father always drove, Katie handed them to him. She then reached inside for Chrissy's child-sized chair.

"He said he had something else he had to do," Katie said. But she couldn't help wondering the same thing. They'd invited Reese to join them for the Fourth of July festivities—the morning parade, an afternoon barbecue at their house and then the fireworks later that night. He'd accepted the invitation to eat with them and watch the fireworks but said he was busy in the morning.

"But he'll miss the parade," Chrissy complained.

Charlie tugged gently on the girl's ponytail. "He can't be with us all the time, bug. He's got his own life and has things to do."

"What things?" Chrissy asked. She hefted her toy rabbit up on her shoulders, holding its legs with her hands as she gave the animal a ride.

"I don't know. Ask your mother," Charlie said.

Katie tossed him a peevish frown, then faced her

daughter. "I don't know for certain, but maybe he doesn't want to be seen by the media."

Chrissy pursed her lips with irritation. "I sure wish those mean old reporters would leave town. Haven't they done enough harm already?"

Katie couldn't help chuckling at her daughter's grown-up words. The child was repeating a sentence Katie had used just last night. It was a reminder that she needed to be careful what she said. Little ears were always listening.

"Maybe you can ask Reese yourself when he comes over to our place for barbecue this afternoon," Katie suggested.

There. That would hopefully cut off any more questions. Katie hated to admit that the day just didn't feel as festive without Reese here. She was missing him as much as her daughter was, and she didn't feel like speculating as to why he couldn't celebrate with them.

"I will ask him," Chrissy said, with a final nod of her head.

As she tromped ahead of them toward the crowded sidewalk, Katie could hear Chrissy muttering something about dads needing to be with their daughters during parades so they could hold them up on their shoulders.

Katie shook her head, trying to ignore Charlie's smile of amusement.

"She acts more and more like her mom every day," he said.

Katie definitely ignored that comment. Keeping her daughter in sight, she hurried toward Main Street, where they looked for a comfortable place to sit and watch the parade.

"Katie! Over here." Megan Marshall waved from where she sat in front of her restaurant with her nine- and six-year-old children, June and Caleb. The thick branches of a sycamore tree provided plenty of cool shade.

"Hi, there," Katie said.

"Why don't you sit with us? There's lots of room," Megan offered.

"This looks like a great place to me. You've got a front-row view," Charlie said.

"Yes, it's premium real estate for a hometown parade. I've had to defend it since early this morning." Megan laughed.

They opened up their lawn chairs and turned to face the street. Chrissy immediately went to join Caleb and June, standing along the sidewalk.

Katie sat in her chair and crossed her legs. "Isn't Jared joining you?"

"No, he and the other hotshots are in the parade."

"Of course." Katie hadn't thought about that. Maybe that was why Reese didn't want to join them. The parade might be a sad reminder that he'd recently lost his own crew.

"Papa, can we have a snow cone, please?" Chrissy asked Charlie, pointing at a vendor on the corner.

Charlie smiled and stood up with help from his cane, then beckoned to Caleb and June. "Of course you can. Come on, kids. What's a parade without a snow cone or cotton candy?"

"You mean we can have both?" Caleb asked in awe.

"No, just one," Megan called after them.

"Aw," the boy said.

"Come on, I'll race you," June said.

The three children took off like a shot.

"Not too fast. Wait for me," Charlie called as he hobbled after them.

The children slowed down for Chrissy's grandpa. They

all held hands and their happy chatter faded as they went to buy their treats.

"Chrissy looks happy today," Megan said.

Katie laughed. "A parade and snow cone will do that to a child."

Megan looked at her critically. "You look happy, too."

"Do I?" Katie didn't know what else to say.

"Yes, you do. Have you seen Reese lately?"

Surprised by the question, Katie reached into her bag for a bottle of water. She popped the lid and took a shallow drink before responding. "Why do you ask?"

"No reason. I just hear that he's been over at your place quite a lot lately."

No doubt the maids were gossiping again. And no doubt the woman was curious about him being Chrissy's daddy.

"He's been doing a few chores for Dad. I think he's about given up on hiding from any news reporters," Katie said.

"Yes, he's been working all over town, from what I've heard. I never knew him when he was in high school, but I understand that he was pretty wild in those days."

"He was, but I think he's changed a lot," Katie conceded, wondering why she felt suddenly territorial.

"Has he asked you out yet?" Megan asked.

Katie gave a nervous jerk. "No, we don't have that kind of relationship."

Her friend tilted her head in confusion. "Don't you? But I thought he was…" She left the sentence hanging.

"What?" Katie pressed.

Megan brushed her comment off with a swipe of her hand. "Oh, nothing. It's none of my business."

No, it wasn't, but Katie didn't think the woman was trying to be unkind. And something settled inside her.

A bit of acceptance that wasn't there before. For the first time, she didn't feel ashamed to admit the truth.

"Yes, Reese is Chrissy's father, but that's all. We're just friends," Katie finally said.

"I still don't see why he hasn't asked you out," Megan said. "You're beautiful and single, with a lot to offer. He'd have to be insane or dead not to notice."

Katie didn't say a word.

"And he's a handsome man. Maybe you should ask *him* out. What have you got to lose?" Megan said.

Just her broken heart.

"No, I'm too old-fashioned to ask a man out. Besides, we're not interested in each other that way."

"Really? Then why do you both light up like Christmas morning every time you see each other? I've noticed how he looks at you."

Katie almost groaned. If Megan weren't such a good friend, she might tell her off for being so blunt.

"It's just your imagination running wild," she said.

"Uh-huh. Yeah, right." Megan eyed her with an expression that said she didn't believe a word.

Katie had absolutely no intention of asking Reese out, but she didn't get to say that because the kids came bouncing back with their snow cones and little miniature American flags Charlie had bought them.

Live marching band music filtered through the air, growing progressively louder. Katie took that opportunity to turn toward the street.

"Look! The parade has started." Chrissy pointed as the high school band came into view.

Katie breathed with relief. She wouldn't have to answer any more of Megan's questions, nor consider her own growing feelings for Reese.

Two majorettes marched in front of the procession.

Wearing red-and-white uniforms with tasseled boots, they carried a wide sign between them with the school name and colors emblazoned across the front.

The bass drums were so loud that they pounded in Katie's chest. Charlie held Chrissy on his lap, while Caleb and June waved their little flags. They all laughed and had a good time, but Katie still felt like something was missing.

Or someone.

Several floats decorated with crepe paper and white pompons passed by, followed by members of the 4-H club mounted on their horses. The blast of a loud horn announced the green Forest Service pumper trucks. When they came into view, the children squealed in delight.

"Look, Mommy! It's Smokey the Bear," Chrissy yelled.

The bear was actually a man wearing a large, furry costume, but the girl didn't care. When Smokey tossed a handful of saltwater taffy at the spectators, Chrissy ran with the other children to snatch it up.

"Don't get in the street," Katie cautioned.

She started to rise from her seat to go and supervise, but Charlie held out a hand.

"I'm the grandpa. I'll go," he announced in a cheerful tone, not seeming at all bothered by his cane and pronounced limp.

The children waved and jumped up and down to get Smokey's attention. And then the bear seemed to take direct aim at Chrissy. The candy peppered her and she busily gathered up so much that she had to use her shirttail to hold it all. She beamed happily as Charlie helped her unwrap a piece to pop into her mouth.

Megan chuckled. "The kids sure are having fun. Last year, Jared played the part of Smokey Bear. Caleb and

June were so excited when they found out it was him in the suit."

Katie nodded, unable to contain a huge smile. "I'll bet they were. Do you know who it is this year?"

Before Megan could answer, a Forest Service truck stopped right in the middle of the street. Jared and Sean hopped off the back and went over to scoop up Chrissy. At first, the girl looked startled, but Jared said something to her and she nodded willingly.

Katie came out of her seat and hurried toward the truck. Where were they taking her daughter?

The two men lifted Chrissy up and Smokey pulled her into his arms. Katie couldn't be sure, but she thought the bear was speaking to Chrissy. The girl nodded several times, a giant grin on her face.

"Give me a big smile," Tessa called from the street, lifting a camera to take a picture.

Katie came up short, realizing the firefighters had perfectly choreographed this photo op. But why had they singled out Chrissy and not some other child?

Her daughter laughed and wrapped her arms around Smokey's neck. She kissed Smokey's furry face and Tessa kept snapping pictures. The photos would be absolutely adorable. And that was when a thought struck Katie. Was it possible that Reese was inside the bear suit? Maybe that was why he'd told them he couldn't join them for the parade. If he was Smokey, it would be a perfect cover for him to participate, yet hide from the media.

"Smokey! Smokey!" The other kids yelled and waved to get the bear's attention. He set Chrissy down and tossed more taffy their way.

Several hotshots stood around the truck, blocking the children from getting too close to the large tires.

Sean lifted Chrissy out of the vehicle and set her safely on the ground beside her mom. "Here she is."

He smiled and raced back to the truck. As soon as he was on board, it started moving again. Smokey waved goodbye. The entire stop hadn't taken more than a minute. It happened so fast that Katie wondered if she'd imagined it all.

"Did you see me with Smokey, Mom?" Chrissy cried happily.

"I did, sweetheart. We'll have to ask Tessa for copies of the pictures," Katie said.

"Yes. I want one for my room."

"What did Smokey say to you?" Katie asked.

Chrissy shrugged. "He just asked if I was having fun and if I wanted to have my picture taken with him. I want to tell Papa about it." The girl ran over to her grandpa, leaving Katie to follow more slowly.

So. The bear might not have been Reese, after all.

"Did you see me, Papa? I got my picture taken with Smokey the Bear," Chrissy said.

Bracing himself against his cane, Charlie smiled and gave her a hearty hug with his free arm. "I did see you, bug. That was quite an honor."

"Yeah, and he gave me this." Chrissy held up a little Smokey the Bear doll that was about eight inches long. Katie hadn't noticed it until now. The bear was a perfect miniature version of the real thing.

"Smokey said he wanted me to remember this day forever. And I will, Papa. I will," Chrissy said.

"That's real nice, bug. I'm glad." Charlie kissed his granddaughter's cheek.

All Katie could do was stare and wonder about the incident. But more and more, she believed Reese had done this. And from the way Chrissy's eyes gleamed with joy,

Katie figured it had been effective and very worth his effort. His thoughtfulness was over the top. He'd made their daughter so happy.

"Can I see your Smokey toy?" Caleb asked. June stood nearby, eyeing the stuffed bear with a bit of envy.

"Sure," Chrissy said and handed it over. The kids each examined the toy, then handed it back.

"That's really cool. I wish I had one," June said.

"Maybe your dad can get you one up at the Forest Service office," Chrissy suggested. "Smokey says we shouldn't play with matches."

"Yeah, our dad is a firefighter, too, so we know all about that," June said.

The kids settled in to watch the rest of the parade. They laughed, talked animatedly together and enjoyed their fill of taffy. Katie didn't have the heart to limit Chrissy to only two pieces. It was a holiday, after all.

"That was really nice for Chrissy," Megan said.

"Yes, it was." Katie sat down and dropped her hands on the armrests of her chair. She smiled but felt a bit dazed.

Megan leaned close and whispered low so none of the children would overhear. "I think we can guess who's playing Smokey this year."

Katie gave an uncertain nod. "I think so."

"He probably wanted to surprise Chrissy. Usually, we don't find out who it is until the parade is over. The firefighters keep it quiet among themselves. Though it's hot inside the bear suit, they love playing with the kids. Most children in these rural towns adore Smokey the Bear."

And Chrissy was no exception. She continued following the bear as the pumper truck moved slowly down the road. Charlie was close by, finally taking her arm to bring her back.

"Reese is a good dad," Megan said.

Katie whipped her head around. Yes, he was a good father, and that was what concerned her so much, but she didn't say so. After he'd left the motel last Sunday evening, Charlie had presented Katie with five crisp one-hundred-dollar bills. Reese had given him the money because he feared Katie might refuse to accept it. He'd told Charlie that it was to help pay bills and buy clothes for Chrissy. He'd promised to provide more financial support, once he found a job in Reno. And that was the crux of the problem. If he was a bad father, it'd be easier for Chrissy to let him go. It'd be easier for Katie, too. And this wasn't getting any easier.

The parade didn't last long, only thirty minutes more. But it turned out to be a highlight of the day. It felt good to see Chrissy so cheerful.

"Now we get to have barbecue and Daddy will be with us. I can't wait to tell him about Smokey the Bear. I'm gonna share some of my taffy with him, too." Chrissy spoke nonstop as they loaded up their lawn chairs and made their way back home.

So. Chrissy didn't know the bear was her father. Maybe Reese would decide not to tell her.

Yes, he had said he would join them for barbecue that afternoon. And Katie couldn't deny having her own feeling of anticipation.

"If you don't mind, just let me off there so no one will see me." Reese pointed down the alley behind the motel.

"Got it. We kept you well hidden from the media today." Jared Marshall turned his Forest Service truck, drove a short way and stopped at the back door to the Ashmores' living quarters.

Reese glanced at the open garage but didn't see Charlie's vehicle inside. No doubt the family hadn't returned from the parade yet. His plan had worked like clockwork. He'd had a blast tossing taffy at Chrissy and then scooping her into his arms while Tessa took their picture. When he'd first seen Katie, she had been sitting nearby, chatting with Megan. Dressed in sandals, capris and a blue shirt, she'd crossed her slender legs and sipped from a water bottle. She'd tucked her long hair up in a bun, with a few tendrils framing her flushed face. She'd looked happy and animated, and completely unaware that he was watching her.

"You need any help getting out of that bear costume?" Jared asked.

Reese shook his head. "Nah, I got this. I'll return it to you tomorrow, after I've had a chance to air it out."

Jared chuckled. "I'm sure the next man who wears the suit will appreciate that."

Reese laughed, too. He'd had so much fun playing the part of Smokey during the parade. And just as Jared had promised, he'd gone incognito, so no reporters knew he was there. He'd already removed the bear head. Most kids' reasoning minds told them that there was a man inside the furry suit, but Reese didn't want to ruin their illusions. The firefighters had treated him like he was one of them, but he really wasn't. Not anymore. Not as long as he couldn't fight wildfires with them.

"See you at the fireworks later tonight," Jared said.

"I wouldn't miss it." Reese wiped a bead of perspiration from his forehead and stepped out of the truck. His hair felt wet and sticky with sweat. Now that the parade was over, he was almost desperate to get out of this itchy, sweltering suit. It must be a hundred degrees inside the costume. No doubt Katie would let him change and wash up before the family barbecue.

Jared pulled away just as Charlie drove down the alley and parked in the garage. Reese paused, eager to see Chrissy. A part of him wondered if he should have hidden the bear suit from her, but another part wanted her to know that he had played the role of Smokey the Bear.

"Daddy!" The girl ran toward him. Her eyes widened when she saw the giant bear head tucked beneath his arm, then she gasped. "You were Smokey the Bear?" she asked with awed disbelief.

He nodded. "I was. Is that okay?"

"Oh, Daddy!" She rushed to him and threw her arms around his waist, then laughed with abandon, brushing at her nose as it was tickled by the furry costume.

Reese hugged his daughter, feeding off her joy. She started babbling about how fun the parade had been and that she now understood why he couldn't go with them. Overall, she was delighted.

"Wait until I tell Caleb and June that my dad was Smokey the Bear. Last year, their dad was Smokey, but they didn't get to have their picture taken with him," she said.

Her mom and grandpa joined them, and Reese almost squirmed beneath Katie's searching gaze. Maybe she didn't like him playing the part of Smokey, or the photo op he'd staged with Chrissy during the parade.

Katie fished around inside her purse and pulled out her cell phone. "May I take a picture of the two of you with the bear head off?"

Reese nodded, grateful she didn't appear to be upset. "Sure! I'd like that, if you promise to send it to my cell phone so I can have a copy."

"Of course."

Within moments he had picked Chrissy up. Like she'd

done during the parade, she wrapped her arms around his neck and smiled for the camera.

Katie clicked several times. "Got it."

Reese set Chrissy on her feet.

"Now I have proof that my dad was Smokey," she said.

Reese chuckled at her exuberance, his chest feeling full and warm. He tugged on her ponytail and spoke in a teasing voice. "Can I get out of this hot bear suit now? I'm broiling in here."

"Of course. Come inside." Charlie unlocked the door to their apartments and opened it wide.

Reese held back, letting the ladies precede him. Chrissy went first. When Katie passed by him, she spoke softly for his ears alone.

"What you did today was really nice. You made Chrissy feel very special. She's so happy. Thank you for that." Then she continued inside, giving him no opportunity to respond.

As Reese went into a back room where he could change and wash the sweat away, he felt an overwhelming happiness. He'd never experienced this before and couldn't explain it. He only knew that this was his family now, for better or worse. Being with them brought him exquisite joy.

So how could he tell them that he'd accepted a job and would be leaving town next week?

That afternoon, as they enjoyed their barbecued hamburgers and hot dogs, and homemade ice cream, Reese's feelings of belonging increased. He longed to tell Katie how he was feeling, but he knew she didn't share his emotion.

When he'd first returned to Minoa, she'd made it clear what her expectations were, and none of them included a relationship with him. He'd done what Katie had asked, getting to know their daughter and having his picture taken with her. In fact, he loved Chrissy with all his heart. But now he had a huge problem on his hands. Because he wanted much more.

Chapter Thirteen

"Where shall we sit?" Katie asked as they arrived at the park that evening. Carrying Chrissy's little folding chair, she perused the congested entrance and wondered if they would be able to find a spot to watch the fireworks.

As long as there were no heavy winds, the spectacle would begin as soon as it was dark. The sun was going down, painting the western horizon with pink and gold.

"How about over there?" Reese pointed to a low hill just inside the park. Although it was crowded with happy families, there were several spaces that might work.

"That's perfect," Charlie said. "Don't wait for me. Hurry and stake out our area. I'll be along shortly."

Toting the lawn chairs, Reese hurried ahead. Chrissy ran beside him, keeping up with his long stride. Carrying a thick blanket, Katie followed with her dad.

Charlie smiled. "They're sure cute together. Almost inseparable."

Yes, and one more reason Katie dreaded Reese's departure. She hated the thought of explaining to Chrissy why her daddy had to leave. She had no idea when that might be and didn't look forward to her daughter's tears.

"While we have a moment alone, I'd like to tell you something," Charlie said.

He drew her away from the foot traffic and they stood together beneath the shade of an elm tree.

Katie looked up at him. "What's on your mind, Dad?"

"I spoke to an attorney yesterday."

She quirked her eyebrows. "What about?"

"He's drawing up the paperwork to make you my full partner in the motel."

"What?" Katie's mind reeled.

Charlie cupped her cheek with his work-roughened hand. "My dear, sweet daughter. You and Chrissy are everything to me. I want you to be happy. You've taken on so many responsibilities at the motel already. It's only right that you officially have a say in how we run it. Besides, when I'm gone, you'll inherit it anyway."

"Oh, Dad. You're way too young to talk about this now." Having lost her mother recently, she didn't want to think about losing Dad, too. Not now, not ever.

"I should live for a long time yet, but you never know. The Lord could take any of us at any time. I want my will and paperwork to be legal and in good order, to make sure you and Chrissy are taken care of. Too many people get caught unprepared. I wanted you to know what plans I'm making and that you never need to be afraid of how you'll provide for Chrissy." He dropped his hand, gazing into her eyes.

Katie hugged him tightly. He smelled of aftershave and peppermint. Familiar scents she would associate with him for as long as she lived. "Thanks, Dad. But I'd rather you stick around for many years to come. I love you so much."

"I love you, too, sweetheart." He drew back and smiled. "There's one more thing I want to say, before it's too late."

She gave a tearful laugh and brushed at her eyes. “Okay. Go ahead.”

He jutted his chin toward where Reese and Chrissy were unfolding the chairs. Or rather, Reese was unfolding them, while Chrissy bounced with excitement.

“You should marry that man.”

Katie snorted. “That’s not gonna happen, Dad.”

“Why not?”

“Because we don’t love each other.”

Charlie leaned closer, his gaze intense. “Are you sure about that?”

Like a blaze of lightning, his words made her realize that no, she wasn’t sure at all. At least, not about her own feelings. But was it love she felt for Reese? The kind of deep, abiding love that would make her heart ache when he left town?

She didn’t want to think about that now. Because if she did, she might not like the answer.

“You want my advice?” Charlie asked.

“No, but I know you’ll give it to me anyway.”

“Ask Reese to stay,” Charlie said.

He didn’t wait for her response but turned and limped toward the spot where Reese was now tickling Chrissy. The girl’s shrill laughter filtered over the buzz of happy chatter. Katie stood there watching them. In her heart of hearts, she had to admit that Reese had changed for the better. He was a good father and a good man. But he needed a job. And she doubted he’d want to stay here in Minoa and help them run the motel. Or would he?

Someone bumped into her, jarring her out of her thoughts.

“Excuse me.” Katie turned.

“Hello, Katie!”

She stood next to Jared Marshall. Megan and their

two kids were beside him, with Sean and Tessa bringing up the rear.

"Hi, there. I'm sorry, I didn't see you," Katie said.

"That's okay. It's pretty crowded tonight. Are you here with your family?" Jared looked around for them.

She nodded and pointed to where Charlie had joined Reese in teasing Chrissy. "Yes, we're all here."

"Reese is with you, too, huh?" Sean asked with a knowing grin.

"Yes." Katie tried not to bristle at the reminder. Her irritation stemmed from something more personal. She didn't want Reese to leave, and it hurt to think that she was so unlovable that he might not want her.

"We're glad to see the two of you together," Tessa said.

Katie bit back a groan. "We're not—"

"Hey! Can we get cotton candy?" Caleb interrupted, pointing at a vendor.

"Maybe later. You've eaten too much junk food today and you didn't finish your dinner," Megan said.

"Aw, but it's the Fourth of July," the boy whined.

Megan gave an embarrassed laugh and grabbed his hand before he could take off into the crowd on his own. "Sorry about this."

"It's okay. I better go. It'll be dark soon." Katie turned and walked toward her family, glad to make an escape.

She skirted around people, threading her way up the hill. By the time she arrived, Charlie and Chrissy were nowhere to be seen. Reese sat alone, guarding their space.

"Where's Chrissy?" she asked, sitting in a chair beside him. Maybe this was a good time to talk about what was really bothering her.

"Charlie took her for cotton candy."

Katie laughed.

"What's so funny?" Reese asked.

"Chrissy didn't finish her dinner. She's eaten too much junk food today."

"Sorry. I didn't think about that."

"It's okay. It's an extra special holiday." She didn't want to get after him or Charlie for spoiling Chrissy. Her daughter wasn't the only one who would never forget this day.

"You love them both very much," he said, a tender expression on his face.

"Yes, they're my whole world." It felt odd and intimate to admit that to this man. Maybe it was because he'd come to mean a lot to her, also.

Ask him to stay.

The words ran through her mind. She opened her mouth to say them out loud but didn't get the chance.

"I need to talk to you about something important," he said.

"Okay. What's on your mind?"

"I have a job offer in Reno," he said.

Her heart gave a powerful thud. "So...so you're leaving?"

"Yeah, I start work next Monday."

A lump formed in her throat. She should have known he'd never be happy working a mundane job at the motel. Reese liked action. So much for asking him to stay. She finally admitted to herself it was what she'd always wanted. For him to remain here with her and Chrissy and be a family for real. But when he'd left town the first time, she'd made a promise to herself. Never again would she wait for a man to love her. If Reese didn't want her, she'd have to accept it and move on with her life. It appeared he'd already made up his mind and his plans didn't include her.

Reese paused, giving Katie time to soak in what he'd told her. To give her time to react.

"Where will you live?" Katie asked.

"My friend said he could put me up, until I find a place of my own. He has a spare room."

"That's nice. I'm glad you found a job. You must be very happy." Her voice sounded forced, as if she was trying to convince him that she was pleased by his news.

"I am. It'll be a new adventure, but I'm up to the challenge."

"Are you sure you don't want to accept Sean's offer to be one of the captains of the Minoa Hotshots?" she asked.

He hesitated. Deep inside, he still loved and respected the profession and regretted that he had to make a change. It couldn't be helped. He'd never been afraid of fighting fires or worried about his own abilities and decision-making skills. Until recently.

"No, I don't think so."

"So, I guess this is it." She looked away and Reese wondered if he'd imagined a flash of disappointment in her eyes.

"Not quite. I'd still like to see Chrissy regularly," he said.

And you. But he bit his tongue to keep from saying that. He didn't know what Katie thought, or how she was feeling. For all he knew, she'd be glad to see him go.

Katie nodded and he caught the flash of her smile in the deepening darkness. "Of course. Chrissy will be glad to hear that."

"And what about you?" he asked, hoping she might give him some sign that she wanted to see him, too.

He had to know where he stood with her. Over the past few weeks, they'd become good friends. And maybe that was best. No one to tie him down. No one that he could hurt the way his father had hurt him. And yet he realized they were way beyond that now. He was Chrissy's daddy. He couldn't go back in time and change that fact. He knew the girl would be deeply hurt when he left.

"Of course. It's been fun to have you visit with us," Katie said. Her voice sounded neutral, with no indication that she might miss him.

"Would you… Would you ever consider moving to Reno?" he asked, trying to feel his way through this discussion without upsetting her.

"No," she answered quickly. "Minoa is my home. Chrissy and I will stay here. Anyway, I could never leave Dad. He needs me to help run the motel."

"Ah, I see." But a part of Reese wished things could be different.

She told him about Charlie making her a full partner in the business. "You probably think running a quiet little motel is boring stuff."

She watched him carefully, as if awaiting his comment.

"Not for you and Charlie," he said. "It's not the kind of work I would choose for myself, though. You're a great asset to him. Really, I mean it."

And he did. He realized he could never ask her to leave Charlie. Her dad was getting older. If Reese couldn't stay and Katie wouldn't leave, then that left them nowhere.

"What about college? I thought you wanted to go to medical school." He couldn't help asking the question.

"I do. I am. I mean, I've already taken a couple of online classes, but I'm majoring in business. I think that will be better for my work at the motel." She gave a little laugh. "Isn't it funny how life changes our priorities?"

"Yeah. Two months ago, I never would have believed I would quit fighting fires."

She startled him by reaching out to squeeze his hand and give him an understanding smile. "It's okay. I had hoped that time might change your mind. It'd be ideal if you could stay here in Minoa. Then you could see Chrissy anytime you like."

A low *kaboom* sounded and he jerked his head up as white fireworks sprayed the night sky. The same kind of sounds he'd experienced on the fire line when giant trees exploded into flame. A chill swept down his spine.

Katie shivered, too, and he swept his jacket over her shoulders.

"Is that better?" he asked.

She nodded. "How did you survive the fire?"

Her question took him off guard. He stared at her for a few moments, then blinked. "I was on my way up the mountain to relieve our lookout when it happened."

"So you weren't with your crew at the time?"

He shook his head, letting the memories rush over him like an icy rain. He spoke softly and she leaned forward to hear him better.

"The wind changed so suddenly, the air growing hotter," he said. "By the time I got up high enough to see what was going on, the fire was raging across the area I'd been working in just minutes before. I never did find Logan."

"Logan?"

"Our lookout. He was supposed to alert us to any changes in the fire, but he never did. At the time, I didn't know why. When I saw the danger, I radioed the crew as fast as I could, but it was too late. I…I stood on that promontory and watched my entire crew die, and I couldn't do a single thing to save them."

"I'm so sorry, Reese. You know it wasn't your fault, right?" Her voice sounded soft with compassion.

He realized tears were running down his cheeks. He brushed them away with an impatient swipe of his hand, feeling embarrassed by this show of emotion. One of the things he'd learned from living with his father was never to cry, because his dad had exploited that weakness.

"It's okay to be sad. Your crew is safe now. God has a plan in mind for each of us. He sees the big picture. Your friends are with Him now." Katie's soft voice soothed his hurt.

"I can almost believe you." He wanted to believe her. He really did.

"The fire investigators found Logan's body hours later," he said. "They believe he fell asleep on the job and didn't wake up in time to warn the crew. He died of smoke inhalation. Because I'd been on my way up the mountain at the time, I was out of the way of the blaze. I'm not a hero at all. I was just doing my job and happened to be the one who survived."

"You're wrong, Reese. You put your life on the line, saving other people's lives and property. You were prepared to take whatever came your way. That makes you a hero in my eyes."

She rested her hand on his arm. Her eyes were filled with warmth and caring. Her words meant so much to him.

More fireworks flashed in the night sky. Reese inwardly flinched with each crackling boom. He'd had no idea the fireworks might affect him this way. Nor did he know why he'd told Katie about the wildfire. And yet it felt good to let it go. To finally get it off his chest and confide in her. He couldn't help wondering if she was right about God loving him. And if that was true, then anything seemed possible. Anything.

He faced her. She sat close beside him and their eyes locked. He felt mesmerized, pulled in by her compassion. As though nothing else mattered but her and making her happy. Before he knew what he was doing, he leaned in and kissed her. Softly. A feathery caress that deepened for several moments. She tasted sweet, like the watermelon they'd eaten an hour earlier. And then she pressed a hand against his chest.

"Reese, I can't." Her voice trembled.

He drew back, embarrassed by what he'd done. He'd felt lost in the moment. What had he been thinking? He was leaving in a few days. He had no right to kiss her.

"Your story is so full of feeling. You should let me write about it," she said.

"No. It won't bring my crew back."

"But it might help other people heal from their own losses," she argued.

"No, I don't want Logan's name dragged through the mud any more than it already has been. They blamed him for the deaths of the crew and I don't believe that's fair. The command team kept us on the fire line way too long. We'd gone over seventy-two hours without sleep and were exhausted. They couldn't flee in time to save their lives. They were all done in."

She sat back and folded her arms. "I'm sorry that happened. To be honest, I should tell you that I've already been writing about you, but I won't publish your story if you don't want me to."

He widened his eyes and a surge of doubt rose up inside him. He'd thought he could trust her. That she wasn't angling to get a story out of him.

"Don't worry, Reese. I'd never publish anything without your permission. I promise." She met his eyes without flinching.

He relaxed, trusting that she would keep her word. "I appreciate that."

They turned as another loud reverberation shook the

air. "I wonder where Chrissy and Charlie are. They're missing the fireworks."

Reese was glad they'd had this talk. It hadn't resolved much, but he felt better. At least they'd agreed that he could come home often for visits. It wasn't as if he was walking out of their lives forever. He'd still get to see Chrissy and Katie now and then. So why did he have such an empty ache deep inside his heart?

Charlie and Chrissy arrived, carrying melting ice cream cones for each of them.

"We were about to give up on the two of you," Reese said as Chrissy handed him a drippy cone.

"We had to stand in line for hours," she exclaimed dramatically.

Charlie chuckled as he sat in his chair and pulled Chrissy onto his lap. "Not quite hours, but the line was pretty long. But I don't mind getting cotton candy and a little ice cream for my granddaughter."

They licked their cones and enjoyed the rest of the evening. When the fireworks ended, they didn't rush to their car. Charlie couldn't move fast, the park was overly crowded and the traffic would be too congested. Instead, they were content to wait until it eased a bit.

As he listened to the happy chatter of his daughter, Reese felt like he belonged here. This was his family. He could no longer think of himself without them. But Katie had her life and he had his. He would visit often, but that wasn't enough anymore. Not for him. He would have told her how he felt, but what good would that do? If he had to leave, it was best to do so without telling her what was in his heart, which would only make things worse.

Chapter Fourteen

Two days later, Katie left the newspaper office and got into her car to drive over to the diner. She'd promised Charlie that she'd bring him some lunch. Chrissy was playing at Caleb and June Marshall's house and Katie would stop and pick her up on her way home.

She'd just had a quarrelsome talk with her editor. Although she'd finished her article on Reese, she was determined not to publish the touching story without his permission. And of course, Tom Klarch hadn't liked that. He'd wheedled and cajoled, trying to convince her to let him print it while the topic was still a current event, but she'd refused. Reese deserved her respect. She didn't want to lose his trust. And Tom had finally agreed to abide by her wishes.

The summer sun glowed brightly as she pulled into the parking lot of the diner. Glancing around, she noticed numerous vehicles and figured the restaurant was busy today. Good thing she'd called ahead to place an order to go.

The bell tinkled above the door as she stepped inside. The pungent scent of chicken curry filled the air along with the conversations of people sitting at tables to eat their lunch.

"Hi, Katie. Your order will be ready in just a few minutes." Cathy Morton waved from behind the cash register.

Knowing that Megan was at home with their children, Katie wasn't surprised to see Cathy waiting tables today. The woman had recently gotten engaged to Rich Wilcox and Megan was planning to cater the wedding.

"I'm not in a big hurry," Katie said.

She sat at the counter to wait, wondering what Reese was doing today. Since he was leaving town tomorrow, he'd spent the last two afternoons with Chrissy, joining them for supper each evening. Tonight would be no different and Katie was planning to prepare something special.

A man walked into the restaurant, bringing Katie out of her thoughts. A short, stocky man wearing a rumpled suit, with dark, shrewd eyes. He held a thick cigar clenched between his teeth. The stinky smoke surrounded her and she waved a hand in front of her face to clear the air.

Katie wasn't sure, but she thought he was the same man she'd seen several weeks ago, his blue sedan parked across the street from Mrs. Watkins's house when Reese had been cleaning up her yard. If that was the case, this was Bruce Miller, the reporter from the National News Registry. He'd been dogging Reese's heels since he came to town. And that made Katie feel defensive.

"You wanting lunch?" Cathy called to Bruce.

"Nope, I'm not buying anything but information," he said, puffing on the cigar. A fog of gray smoke filtered through the air. Several people sitting nearby coughed and glared in disapproval.

Cathy came to stand in front of him, looking stern as

she placed her hands on her waist. "You're not from Nevada, are you?" she said.

"Nope, I'm from Colorado. Why do you ask?"

"Because if you were from Nevada, you'd know better than to smoke in a public place. It's against the law. Before I can give you anything, I'm gonna have to ask you to put that cigar out." She pointed at a sign on the wall that read No Smoking!

"Sorry." He dropped the stogie onto the floor and crushed it out with the sole of his shoe.

Cathy's eyes widened with outrage. Reaching over to a canister on the counter, she whipped out a couple napkins and handed them to him. "Clean that up, please."

The man rolled his eyes and pursed his fat lips. From his demeanor, he looked like he was about to refuse. But Cathy glared a hole right through him, so he bent down and cleaned up the mess. When he was done, Cathy shot out her hand to take the blackened napkins before tossing them into the trash.

"Now, what do you want?" she asked in a brittle tone.

Whew! If Bruce Miller wanted information, he was going about it the wrong way.

Katie hid a smile of amusement. Cathy was always easygoing and polite. But this reporter had been nothing but rude since he walked through the door.

"Anyone here know Reese Hartnett?" Bruce called to the room.

Everyone turned to look at him and Katie stiffened. No one said a word, their dark glares speaking volumes.

"What do you want with Reese?" Frank, the cook, came out from behind the kitchen partition, drying his burly hands on a clean dish towel.

"I just want to ask him a few questions, that's all. I was

wondering where he's staying." Bruce's voice sounded a tad wheedling.

Cathy leaned against the counter. "Who are you, and what business do you have with Reese?"

"I work for the National News Registry. I just want to meet and talk with him," Bruce said.

"So, you're a reporter." Cathy spoke as if she'd just said a dirty word.

"Yes, and I'd like to interview Mr. Hartnett."

A deathly silence filled the restaurant. In the past, Reese had a bad reputation. He'd been a hoodlum who had caused a lot of trouble in town. But since his return, he'd done nothing but good works. He'd tried to undo his wrongs and everyone had been talking about him. Now Reese was a member of their community. They were protective of him.

"I don't think any of us has anything to say to you about Reese," Katie said.

A subtle sneer curved the man's lips, reminding Katie of a slithering snake.

"There might be something in it for you, too," he said.

She turned away, repulsed by the stench of cigar smoke. "No, thanks."

"If you're not gonna buy something, I'll have to ask you to leave," Cathy said.

Bruce stood there, looking around the room, searching the customers for one friendly face. But there weren't any. They scowled at him until he finally turned and walked out.

"Whew! I'm glad that stink is gone." Cathy waved a hand.

Katie wasn't so sure Reese was out of trouble, though. Standing up, she peered out the wide, sparkling windows. Bruce stood in the parking lot, speaking to a teenage girl.

When she pointed toward Cove Mountain, Katie knew the jig was up. Most everyone knew by now that Reese was staying at their cabin, but she hadn't seen Bruce around town for a couple weeks. Maybe he had just recently returned. She had little doubt the teenage girl had just told him where Reese was staying.

"Here you go, honey." Cathy handed Katie a brown bag with her sandwiches inside.

"Thanks." She handed over some bills to pay for her food, then zipped out the door. Thankfully, she was driving Charlie's truck. Hopping inside, she tossed the bag of food onto the seat and dialed Reese's cell number. No answer. Not surprising if he was up at the cabin, where he wouldn't have reception. She had a mission right now. Something more important than eating lunch. She planned to race over to Megan's house, pick up Chrissy from her playdate and then hightail it up to Cove Mountain. Hopefully Reese was there and she could warn him. Just one thought occupied her mind. She had to get to the cabin and warn Reese before Bruce Miller obtained a truck or attempted to drive up the mountain with his car.

Reese stood at the gas station on Main Street, pumping fuel into the old wood truck he'd borrowed from Charlie. He was leaving tomorrow and wanted to return the vehicle with a full tank.

Wiping his brow, he missed his baseball cap. The reporters had stopped bothering him, so he'd let down his guard. He'd forgotten the cap that morning when he'd gone over to the Shurtzes' place to rebuild their chicken coop. He'd finished the chore and planned to head over to the diner for a little lunch and a cold drink. Then he was going to the motel. If he had to leave tomorrow, he wanted to make the most of this afternoon. As a new employee, he didn't know yet when he'd get a couple days off work and was going to miss his family more than he could say.

The gas hose clicked off and Reese went inside to pay his bill. Bill Olson, the owner of the gas station, shook his hand. "You're a good man. I'm sorry I misjudged you," he said.

Reese stared in confusion. He'd never wronged this man. Maybe he'd been listening to gossip.

At the cash register, Reese picked up a copy of the *Minoa Daily News*. The headline immediately caught his eye: Local Hero is the Lone Survivor.

A sick feeling settled over him as his gaze darted to the byline.

Katie Ashmore.

He scanned the words, reading the article. It discussed the wildfire that had killed his hotshot crew and included numerous private details he had shared with Katie. He had no doubt she'd written the story.

With an angry huff, he wadded the paper with his hands, then thought better of it. Spreading out the creases, he paid for it and his gas, then walked out to his truck and tossed the paper onto the seat.

He never saw this coming. In a rush, everything he'd told Katie came back to him with vivid details. Their special conversation during the fireworks when he'd confided in her. The numerous moments when they'd laughed as they watched their daughter do something funny. The overwhelming love he'd felt toward both of them.

Yes, he realized it now. He loved them all. Katie, Chrissy and Charlie. He wanted to be with Katie. But right now, he felt so betrayed. So used. He'd thought he could trust her. After all, she was the mother of his child. They were more than friends. Weren't they?

Apparently not. What a fool he'd been, telling her such personal things. Asking her not to publish the story she'd written. The night of the fireworks, she'd promised not to. He didn't need this. Long ago, he'd had his fill of lies and suspicion. His father had taught him not to trust. To keep his feelings bottled up inside. But Reese had let down his guard. He was done with this one-dog town for good. When he left, he was never coming back.

With stiff movements, he climbed into his truck and started up the engine. Putting the vehicle into gear, he pulled into traffic and headed toward Cove Mountain. He'd pack up his duffel bag this very afternoon, drive the truck over to the motel, leave the keys in it so Charlie could find them, and head out of town as fast as he could go. He'd hitched rides before and he could do it again. He didn't want to say goodbye to Katie, or Charlie, or even Chrissy.

Ah, that wasn't true. He couldn't leave without seeing Chrissy one last time. She was innocent in all of this mess. And that meant he'd have to see Katie, too. But he'd keep it short. Kiss Chrissy, tell her he loved her, try not to tell Katie what he really thought of her lies, then beat it out of town before he could change his mind. He didn't need this family. He didn't need anyone.

Gripping the steering wheel, Reese realized that wasn't true, either. Before he'd returned, he had believed it, but not anymore. Since he'd gone to church and fed off Katie's undying faith, he'd finally exercised the power of prayer. He couldn't deny the closeness he now felt toward his Heavenly Father. No matter who betrayed him, turned their back on him, hated or reviled him, he was never alone. He always had God by his side. He knew that now more than ever and couldn't go back in time and pretend that he didn't. But that didn't change the fact that Katie had lied to him.

Chapter Fifteen

"Where is Daddy?" Chrissy asked for the third time.

She stood with Katie outside the cabin on Cove Mountain. They'd arrived ten minutes earlier. After chasing a chipmunk around the yard, Chrissy had gotten bored.

"I'm not sure, sweetheart."

Standing beneath the shade of a tall pine tree, Katie scanned the area, looking for some sign of Reese. When she hadn't seen her father's old wood truck parked out front, she'd figured he must be gone. She'd knocked on the door anyway. When no one answered, she'd turned the knob. It wasn't locked, but she didn't feel good about going inside when he wasn't there.

"We'll give your dad fifteen more minutes and then go home. I'll try to call him again as soon as we get into a service area," Katie said.

"But I want to see him," Chrissy said.

So did Katie. And not just because she wanted to tell him that Bruce Miller was hunting for him. She couldn't forget the tender kiss they'd shared in the park, nor the way he'd brushed his hand over her arm in a gentle caress. The way he always said just the right words to make her feel better. The way he made her laugh. He'd been so much help to Charlie and had made Chrissy so happy. Katie admired Reese's kindness and generosity and the way he always pitched in to help someone in need. He truly had changed.

She should go home. He'd be joining them for dinner later, but she feared what might happen if Bruce Miller arrived at the cabin while Reese wasn't home. With the door unlocked, she wouldn't put it past the reporter to go inside and rifle through his belongings.

The sound of an engine brought her head around.

"There he is!" Chrissy jumped up and down, pointing as Charlie's old wood truck appeared.

Reese sat in the driver's seat. When he saw them, he frowned. Katie barely noticed, feeling a leap of joy. She told herself it was relief that she'd get to warn him about Bruce Miller, but she knew that wasn't all. She got this buoyant feeling every time she saw him. She cared deeply for this man. It did no good to deny it any longer.

He pulled into the graveled driveway and parked behind her vehicle. Katie expected him to hop out and hurry over to them like he usually did, but he sat there staring at her for several moments. His jaw was locked, his eyes creased with anger. He seemed upset.

"Daddy!" Chrissy sprinted toward the truck.

Reese stepped out, carrying a newspaper with him. He smiled at Chrissy, but it didn't reach his eyes. Yes, he was definitely troubled by something.

"Hi, bug." He spoke in a monotone voice.

Katie noticed he used Charlie's nickname for the little girl. Even though he'd been here a short time, it felt as though he belonged with them.

"We've been waiting for you," Chrissy said.

"You have, huh?" But he didn't touch her. He didn't hug her, pick her up or tickle her like he usually did.

"I'm so glad you're here," Katie said. "Bruce Miller was in town. I think he knows where you're staying."

Reese looked right through her. Katie walked toward him, but he brushed past her.

"That shouldn't be a problem, since I'm leaving." His voice sounded brusque and his shoulders were tense.

Katie stared as he went inside the cabin. She and Chrissy followed him, watching from the doorway as he tossed the newspaper onto the sofa. He started stuffing his clothes and other belongings into his duffel bag.

"What are you doing?" Katie asked, confused by his actions.

"I told you. I'm leaving."

Katie blinked. "Right now?"

"Yes."

"But I thought you were coming over to the motel tonight, to share supper with us. We have a little celebration planned. I thought you were leaving in the morning. Dad was even going to drive you into Reno."

"That's not gonna happen now."

Why wouldn't he look at her? What was going on? From his stiff body language, she knew he was fuming about something.

"Are you leaving early because of Bruce?" she asked.

"No."

Chrissy reached up to take her hand and Katie realized she sensed Reese's hostility, too. He obviously wasn't happy to see them.

"You can stay at the motel tonight. Bruce won't find you there," Katie offered.

He snorted. "No, thanks. You've done enough already."

"Reese, what's going on? I don't understand."

"Maybe this will explain." He picked up the newspaper and tossed it at her.

She caught the paper in midair, surprised by his rudeness, but then she saw the cause. Plastered across the front was a picture of Reese, Chrissy and Katie playing together in the leaves over at Mrs. Watkins's house. The headline left nothing to the imagination. A quick scan of the accompanying article told Katie all she needed to know.

In a rush, she realized what had happened. Tom Klarch had promised not to publish her story, but he'd lied. Reese didn't know that, of course. He thought she had gone behind his back and…

"Reese, I didn't know about this," she said.

"Didn't you?" he challenged with a lift of his head. "The story includes private details. Things I haven't told anyone but you. No one else could have written that story. It has your name on it."

She stepped into the room, leaving Chrissy standing in the doorway. She hated for the little girl to witness this scene, but it couldn't be helped. Reese was leaving. Right now. She might never get another chance to set the record straight, or tell him how she really felt about him.

"Yes, I wrote the story. The night of the fireworks, I told you about it, but I promised you I wouldn't publish it and I didn't. Tom must have gone into my computer at work without my permission. Since I only work there part-time, I have a very old machine that's not password protected."

"Is that right?" Reese sounded angry, his voice rising.

"Yes, it's the truth," she said.

"You really expect me to believe that?" He met her eyes, his suspicious expression telling her he wasn't convinced.

"Yes, I do."

He slashed the air with his hand. "No more lies, Katie. How can I believe you?"

Chrissy flinched at his loud voice. That did it. Katie stared at him, her own anger boiling up inside.

"After all the bad things you've done in your life, who are you to accuse me of lying?" she asked, her own voice escalating several octaves.

"I never lied to you, Katie. I never made you any promises. I didn't even know about Chrissy until recently. Did you make that up, too, so you could get a story out of me?"

A gasp came from Chrissy. Katie whirled around in time to see the girl's face turn white. Her eyes flooded with tears and her chin quivered. She looked at her father, then at her mother, as though trying to comprehend what was going on. A small sound of distress came from the back of her throat.

"Chrissy, I'm sorry…" Reese didn't get to finish. The girl let out a sob, turned and ran from the cabin, racing down the thin trail leading into the forest.

Katie whirled on Reese. "Now look what you've done. You promised you'd never hurt her."

"I'm sorry, Katie. I didn't mean it," he said.

But it was too little, too late. He'd said the words and they were out there now. He couldn't take them back. And like always, Katie would be the one to smooth it over, if that was possible.

"You can believe whatever you want, but I've never lied to you. Not ever," she said. "Now, I've got to go find Chrissy and do more damage control. I think it's best if you leave town as soon as possible."

She turned and headed toward the trail leading into the trees. She loved Reese, but she'd been wrong about him. She thought he'd changed for good this time, but he hadn't. He'd hurt both her and Chrissy. There was no future for them together. It was all over. She'd been a fool to ever believe they might be able to work things out and become a real family. Now it was too late. All hope of reconciling their relationship was completely lost.

As she ran across the road toward the mouth of the hiking trail, something caught Katie's eye. A plume of black smoke rose upward from the trees at the bottom of the mountain. She paused.

"Katie, wait! I'll go with you," Reese called to her from the doorway.

She didn't want to stop. She wanted to find Chrissy and go home. She was good and mad and wanted nothing to do with Reese ever again. But she'd never seen smoke on the mountain before. It couldn't be from a campfire. This side of the mountain was all private property. And they hadn't had a lightning storm in months. So what was the cause?

Reese joined her, but she barely noticed. In spite of the hot day, a shiver swept down her spine.

"Is that a fire?" She pointed.

He hurried back to the cabin and returned momentarily with a pair of binoculars before gazing through them. The fire appeared to be over by the lake, which meant it hadn't blocked the main road. Yet.

"Yes, it's a fire, and it's growing right before my eyes," he said.

He studied the sky above. Then he held up a hand, as though feeling the wind. "We've got to get out of here, right now."

Absolute terror washed over Katie. His words only confirmed her worst fears. Somehow, a wildfire had started on the mountain. She didn't need anyone to tell her that they'd be trapped up here if they didn't leave soon.

"Chrissy! Chrissy!" she yelled.

Together, they ran into the trees, following the hiking trail for several minutes. Katie scanned the dense foliage, looking for any sign of her daughter. She had no idea how far Chrissy might have run. The child could have gone to the meadow, or over by the footbridge that crossed the creek, or one of her other favorite spots in the forest. She could be anywhere and they didn't have time to check each place.

"I don't know where to look," Katie cried. "Oh, Reese! Where is she?"

Reese caught the tremor of fear in Katie's voice. She sounded the way he was feeling inside. They had to find Chrissy. He was an experienced wildfire fighter and had gauged the wind speed and the incendiary location of the blaze. By his calculations, the cabin was directly in the path. If they got into their vehicles and left now, they would have just enough time to make it to the main road and safety. But they couldn't leave without Chrissy. Not without his little girl.

"Chrissy!" he called, bolting through the trees. The pungent scent of wood smoke grew stronger. The fire was undoubtedly spreading, growing in size, encompassing the mountain.

Where was she? He never should have accused Katie of lying. He knew Chrissy was his child. This was his fault. If only he hadn't let his hurt and fears get the better of him. He'd felt so betrayed by Katie that he'd struck out in anger, trying to wound her the way his father had wounded him. No wonder Chrissy had run into the forest. And now, they might all lose their lives because of it.

Because of him.

No! He couldn't accept that. He couldn't lose his family. Not when he'd so recently found them. He knew Katie wouldn't have published his story without his permission. He'd met her editor and realized the man had gone behind her back.

They kept running, calling Chrissy's name, searching the thick brush for any sign of her. Reese prayed, deep inside his heart. Begging the Lord to save them. To give him one more chance to make this right.

They reached the open meadow where Reese had seen several deer grazing just days earlier. A beautiful, alpine glen surrounded by thick, heavy timber. Now the summer's baking heat had turned the tall grass to dry tinder. If the fire reached this spot, all would be lost. The whole place would blow up like a lighted torch. Unless…

Please, God. Help us.

He prayed again. And that was when a glow of insight flooded his mind. A still, small voice whispered deep within him what he should do.

He reached for Katie's arm and pulled her toward him. "Katie, we've got to go back to the cabin."

She looked at him like he was daft. "Are you crazy? I'm not going anywhere until I find Chrissy."

"Neither am I, but I know without a doubt that we've got to go back," he said.

Billows of smoke darkened the sky. A dull roar filled the air—the sound of flames consuming everything in their path. The fire wasn't close yet, but with this wind speed, it would be soon. If he was going to save their lives, he didn't have much time left.

"Please, Katie. Trust me. I know what I'm doing. I need to start a backfire and I need some tools to do that. I need you to be strong right now and keep it together a little while longer. Come with me. Please," he said, unwilling to leave her there alone.

She hesitated, her eyes wide with panic and doubt. She was trembling with fear and shock. The last thing he needed right now was a hysterical woman on his hands. Short of tossing her over his shoulder and carrying her back to the cabin kicking and screaming, he didn't know what he would do if she refused. And if his plan didn't work and they couldn't find Chrissy…

No, he couldn't think like that. He had to stay positive. Had to fight for their lives. They would find Chrissy. They must!

"All right," Katie said, her voice wobbling.

He took her hand and they ran back the way they'd come. Along the trail, rocks and gravel rolled beneath their feet. Running up the mountain was more taxing than coming down. Reese's breath came fast and hard; his lungs and thighs were burning. Katie must be feeling the same, but he didn't dare let her stop. He pulled her along and they made it in record time.

"Chrissy!" Katie yelled.

The girl stood in front of the cabin, her eyes red from crying. She clutched her compass in her hands, looking frightened and forlorn.

"Mommy! Daddy! There's smoke in the sky. I thought you'd left me."

"Oh, Chrissy. We'd never leave you, sweetheart. Not ever." Deep relief flooded Reese, but he didn't have time to say more.

"Stay here," he called as he raced inside the cabin for his leather gloves, fire shelter and a lighter.

Mother and daughter stared at him as he ran to the shed and threw open the wooden door. In the dim shadows, he found the Pulaski he'd borrowed from Charlie's shed and set against the wall weeks earlier when he'd used it to clean up the yard at the cabin. A Pulaski was a wildfire fighter's most prized hand tool, which combined an ax and an adze in one head. Grabbing the handle, he barreled outside again. He brushed the palm of his free hand against Katie's and Chrissy's cheeks and gave them a tender smile, trying to convey his love for them. Fearing they no longer trusted him, he knew he had to say something to them. Otherwise, they might not obey his commands. And he needed them to follow him right now. He also needed to apologize, in case this was their last moment together.

"I'm sorry for what I said earlier. I didn't mean it. Please forgive me." Then he looked at Katie. "Take Chrissy's hand and don't let go for a moment. Follow me."

Carrying the Pulaski, he turned and ran, glancing over his shoulder to ensure they were with him. He would never leave them. Never again. No matter what. He knew now what was most important in his life. He knew what he wanted. He longed to tell them, but there wasn't time. He had to save them first.

Within minutes, they reached the meadow. The growl of the fire had amplified and the heat increased, telling him that the flames were advancing faster than he had first thought. Churning smoke rose from the forest like a black beast.

He positioned Katie and Chrissy along the edge of the woods, at the farthest point away from where he thought the fire would break over them. They stood right near the trail leading up to the cabin. If he failed with his plan, they could run for it, but he doubted they'd ever make it back. Neither man nor beast could outrun a fire when it was on the move. And if they did make it to the cabin, the fire would find them there.

"Stand here and don't move unless I tell you to," he yelled over the increasing noise.

"Can't we go to the lake?" Katie cried, holding Chrissy close.

The girl pressed her face against her mom's abdomen, but she peeked out at Reese, her eyes filled with tears, her face pale with fright.

"The lake is three miles away and the fire is blocking our route. Stay with me. I don't have time to explain, but we're gonna be okay. I promise." And he meant every word. So help him, he did. He'd never stop fighting to save them, not until his dying breath.

Katie nodded, her eyes wide with terror. She huddled there with Chrissy and their trust meant everything to Reese.

He set to work, building a fire line around the perimeter of the meadow. Without fuel, the fire would burn away from them. He used the lighter to set a backfire in the dried pine grass. A whoosh of air whipped the flames to life, fanning them across the clearing. Sprinting back and forth, Reese worked hard to keep the fire from jumping his fire line and getting into the tall trees beyond. His lungs burned from the smoke and he coughed. His muscles cramped and screamed for him to stop, but he kept moving. He knew what was at stake. His daughter's life. And Katie, the love of his life.

Scraping back the grass to mineral soil, he toiled until the fire he'd set had burned the whole meadow. With no more fuel to consume, the flames died out. The blackened earth steamed as he raced back to his family. And that was when Reese became aware of the sound of a freight train rushing toward them.

He turned, then shuddered. The wildfire had finally arrived. He could see red flames flickering among the tree trunks at the edge of the clearing and dancing in the canopies of tall pines and Douglas fir.

For a scant moment, his PTSD threatened to take over. With determination born of faith, he turned his back on the fire and refused to allow his fears to undermine his purpose. He couldn't lose it now. Katie and Chrissy were depending on him.

"Reese!" Katie cried. She stared at the scene, her face drawn with terror.

"Don't look at it, Katie. Look at me." He beckoned to her.

She gazed at him. Only him. Holding on to Chrissy, she pulled the child with her, accepting Reese's outstretched hand as he took them to the middle of the burned-out meadow. Using the Pulaski, he quickly cleared away the blackened grass. Blasts of hot air struck him as he shook out his fire shelter, a safety device shaped like a sleeping bag and made out of fire-resistant materials. Used as a last resort, it was large enough for one man…or a petite woman and child. It couldn't withstand sustained contact with flames, but it sure could protect them in a short-lived grass fire.

He helped Katie and Chrissy to lie down inside the shelter, their feet toward the blaze. Because there wasn't room for him to crawl inside, too, he hugged up against the outside of the shelter, pressing his face, arms and legs beneath it to give him some protection from the intense temperatures.

"Daddy, it's too hot. I can't breathe," Chrissy yelled.

"Press your face against the ground and cover your nose and mouth with your hand. Breathe through your nose. Air near the earth will be the coolest. And whatever you do, don't get up until I tell you to," he yelled back.

They lay just as he instructed. He'd done everything

he could to protect them from the intense heat, taking the brunt of it himself. The roar of the fire filled his ears. His exposed back felt like it was aflame, his civilian clothes providing little protection against the blasts of superheated air. How he wished he was wearing his fire-resistant Nomex shirt and pants. He wanted to scream with pain, but he didn't. He wanted to get up and run, but he knew that would mean certain death. Instead, he gritted his teeth and kept his face against the ground. Wearing his leather gloves, he gripped folds of the fire shelter so he wouldn't be tempted to rise up and breathe scorching air that would burn his lungs.

They lay like that for what seemed like hours. Reese could hear Chrissy crying and it tore at his heart. And yet, in spite of the noise and pain, in the midst of the broiling fire, he felt completely calm. Certain he had done all that he could for them. He turned the rest over to God, finally prepared to accept the Lord's will. And when the fire passed, Reese raised his head and looked around.

"Katie, Chrissy, are you all right?" he asked.

Slowly, they opened the shelter and lifted their stiff bodies to sit up. They looked around at the ruined forest, their faces, clothes and hair blackened by dirt, smoke and ash. Thin drafts of smoke drifted from tree branches devoid of leaves or any sign of life. But a sense of overwhelming gratitude filled Reese's heart. They were alive. They were safe. Because God had answered his prayers.

Chapter Sixteen

"Reese, we're alive." Katie spoke with amazement, her voice sounding thin and watery to her ears. She couldn't believe they'd made it through the firestorm.

"Is it over?" Chrissy lifted her head and looked around, her expression still drawn with fear.

"Yes, sweetheart. It's over. Are you both okay?" Reese moved stiffly, grimacing as though in pain. Katie wasn't surprised. A glance at her watch told her that they'd been lying on the ground for over an hour.

He gave a deep, hacking cough as Chrissy nodded, setting her long ponytail dancing. Both Reese and Katie inspected her closely. Except for being covered by soot, the girl looked completely unharmed.

Tears of gratitude filled Katie's eyes. "Yes, I think we're all right. You did it. You saved our lives, Reese."

He nodded, his shoulders slumping with relief. He looked at the burned remnants of the scorched woods and gave a disbelieving laugh. "No, I didn't save us. The Lord did. He pulled us through."

Katie couldn't believe her ears. His words were completely unexpected. She never would have believed that Reese would give credit to God for anything.

"Reese! Katie! Is that you?"

They turned and stared toward the west, where the trail leading up to the cabin should have been. It was no longer visible beneath the macabre ruins of blackened trees and bushes. Two men stood there, dressed in full wildfire-fighting gear. They each gripped a Pulaski. One of them removed his red helmet.

Sean Nash!

"Man! Are we ever glad to find all of you safe. We figured you were lost in the fire." Jared Marshall pushed back his white helmet as he smiled widely and walked toward them.

"Not half as happy as we are to see you," Reese said, his voice sounding hoarse.

He coughed again, and Chrissy did, too. Katie felt a heaviness in her lungs and thought they must all need treatment for smoke inhalation.

She stood, her legs limp and shaky. She pulled Chrissy up with her and hugged her tightly. Tears of happiness ran down her face. They were safe. When Reese had asked her to trust him, she had prayed for help and felt strongly that she should follow him. The Lord hadn't failed them today. They had so much to be grateful for.

"Look at the forest, Mommy. It's all burned up," Chrissy said with amazement.

"Yes, but it will recover. All that matters right now is that we survived," Katie assured her.

Jared and Sean helped Reese to stand. He stumbled and she realized he was having difficulty walking.

"Your back is badly burned. Does it hurt?" Jared asked. The man lifted Reese's tattered shirt and studied his blistered skin.

Reese groaned, his face twisted in agony. "Yes, very much."

"I'm sorry for the pain, but that's a good sign. No third-degree burns. Just superficial blisters. They'll be mighty painful for a while, but you should be okay."

Reese coughed again. "How…how did you find us?"

"Mrs. Murdoch lives a quarter of a mile down the road. She saw the smoke and called to report the fire," Jared said. "The hotshot crew is out building line now. Because we had an early warning, we think we'll have the fire contained soon."

Reese smiled with cracked lips. His face, hands and arms were dotted with angry red burns. No wonder he was in pain.

Neither Katie nor Chrissy had any significant wounds. Because Reese had given them the fire shelter, he'd taken the heat and had sustained some ugly injuries. Her heart went out to him. She couldn't believe what he'd sacrificed for them. And that reminded her that Jesus had suffered for mankind. His excruciating torment in the Garden of Gethsemane and then His death upon the cross had never struck her with such meaning until now. And she knew deep within her heart that if Christ could forgive all her failings, then she must also forgive others.

She must forgive Reese.

"Are you really okay?" she asked as she reached for him. She found herself shaking like a leaf, weak and exhausted. They'd all been through a horrible ordeal.

"I'm in a lot of pain, but I'll be fine." He spoke through gritted teeth, giving her a half smile that looked more like a grimace. "I still can't believe we survived. The Lord brought us through, Katie. He saved us."

His words touched her heart. Reese was so brave. So strong and capable. Even though he must be hurting, he was still trying to be strong for them.

Sean got on his radio, calling for help. Tessa soon arrived with a first aid kit. By the time she had bandaged the patches of burns on Reese's body and treated them each for smoke inhalation, four other men appeared with a stretcher.

"Let's move it out." Sean waved his hand in the air.

The men loaded Reese on the stretcher and carried him up the hill, with Tessa close by to lend medical aid. As Katie took Chrissy's hand and followed at a slower pace, with Jared by their side, a trillion thoughts zipped through her mind. So many words she wanted to say to Reese. Words of appreciation, love and trust. But now wasn't the time. They needed care. Before she did anything else, Katie wanted Chrissy checked out by a doctor. First things first.

They arrived at the cabin and she was stunned to find it still standing, though the surrounding area had been scorched by flames.

"How is it possible the cabin didn't burn?" she asked.

Jared shrugged, as if the answer was obvious. "You cleared a defensible area around it."

Katie's mouth dropped open. "Reese did that, weeks ago when he first arrived."

"Well, it made a big enough difference that we were able to save the place." Jared nodded as the men set Reese's stretcher on the ground.

Harlie and Dean headed down the hill to retrieve a Forest Service truck.

"Should we have stayed at the cabin instead of lighting the backfire down in the meadow?" Katie asked the men.

She thought about all that they'd gone through to survive the burnover and wondered if it had been necessary.

Sean shook his head. "No, definitely not. The cabin might have burned if Reese hadn't set the backfire. The combination of burning up the fuel in the meadow and clearing a defensible area around the cabin made all the difference. The backfire probably caused the wind direction to shift, taking the fire south of the cabin instead of directly over top of it. It also slowed the main fire, giving us time to set up our pumper trucks to fight the flames. Without Reese setting the backfire, I believe the cabin would have burned. If you had taken refuge here, you would have died."

Katie covered her mouth with one hand, realizing that Reese had definitely known what he was doing. He truly was a hero and had saved their lives. His actions had saved their cabin, too. The Lord had truly been with them, guiding Reese every step of the way.

She looked at him again. Lying flat, he had his face pressed against the stretcher, his mouth and nose covered by an oxygen mask. His eyes were closed, which frightened her.

Tessa touched her arm, whispering softly for her ears alone. "I gave him something for the pain, but it's not strong enough. He's hurting pretty bad."

Oh, no! Katie hated to think of what he was going through. Crouching beside him, she touched his shoulder gently with one finger. "Reese?"

He opened his eyes. He must have seen her worried expression, because he gave her a wan smile through the oxygen mask. Thankfully, Katie and Chrissy seemed to be breathing well enough on their own. And they had Reese to thank for that.

"I'll be okay. I won't accept anything less," he said, his words muffled by the mask.

"I'm so grateful for what you did today. I can't even find words to thank you enough," she said.

"Me, too, Daddy. You're my hero," Chrissy said. The girl leaned forward and gently kissed his forehead.

He smiled and lifted a hand to reach for them but then let his arm fall limply to his side. He was in no condition to touch anything right now. "I never wanted to be a hero, but I admit I kind of like being your hero."

Katie laughed, thinking how hard he had fought to stay out of the limelight. Within the past two months, he'd survived two firestorms. "I hope you'll let me write a story about what happened to us today. It'll be the last article I ever write for the *Minoa Daily News*."

He arched a singed eyebrow. "The last one?"

"Yes. As soon as I'm feeling better, I'm going into the office to give Tom Klarch our story and my resignation. I just quit. I won't work for that man anymore."

Reese gave one stiff nod. "I know you never gave him permission to publish the article about my hotshot crew. And honestly, your story was a beautiful tribute to their lives. I'm sorry I ever doubted you. From now on, you can write whatever you want. I trust you completely, Katie."

"And I trust you," she said.

He turned his head slightly, his gaze locking with hers. "Do you really mean that?"

She nodded. "I do."

"That means a lot to me." He laid his cheek against the stretcher and shut his eyes.

She rested a hand next to him, longing to be close to him. In fact, she was worried sick. What if the fire had been too much? What if his burns were worse than they thought and he had irreparable damage? What if he'd inhaled too much smoke and was unable to recover? They'd shared so much over the past weeks. She would love him no matter what, but she couldn't lose him. Not now. Not after all that they'd been through.

"Okay, load him in the truck," Sean said.

Katie stepped back, giving the men room to pick Reese

up off the stretcher. She hadn't even been aware that they'd returned with the vehicle.

Reese cried out and she flinched, knowing they were hurting him. But it couldn't be helped. With no ambulance in this small town, they slid him into the back of Sean's hotshot truck so he could lie facedown on the seat. Tessa propped his head with a blanket.

"I've used the radio to get word to your father that you're safe. He's been worried about you. He'll drive your car and meet you at the hospital in Carson City," Tessa said.

Carson City had the nearest medical facility, thirty miles away.

"Thank you," Katie said.

Jared helped Katie and Chrissy climb into the front seat, then got in and drove them off the mountain. They spoke very little, the air permeated by repeated coughing as they tried to clear the smoke out of their lungs.

"Mrs. Murdoch said she saw a blue sedan drive by her place a few minutes before she saw the smoke from the fire," Jared said from the driver's seat.

"Oh?" Katie remembered that Bruce Miller drove just such a vehicle. Was it possible that he'd been up on the mountain, after all? She would never dare drive a car up on Cove Mountain. At the very least, the rugged roads would damage the muffler and throw the tires out of alignment. And that was if you took it slow. Bruce Miller didn't strike Katie as the type of person to be anything but rude and impatient. But if he had damaged his car, it served him right for all the trouble he'd caused.

"Since this is a private area, Mrs. Murdoch was suspicious of any strangers on the mountain, so she took down the license plate number," Jared continued. "I passed it on to Chief Sanders. The police will track it down and conduct some interviews. Once the investigation team discovers what started this fire, we may find out that the owner of the car was responsible."

Katie nodded, thinking about the stinky cigars Bruce liked to smoke. She wouldn't be surprised if he had tossed one out his car window and it had ignited the flames.

"What do you have there?" she asked Chrissy, when she noticed she held something in her hands.

Chrissy held it up. "My compass. When I ran into the forest, I saw the smoke and got scared. I was lost for a while, but then I prayed and remembered what Daddy had taught me. I used my compass to find my true north, and that led me back to the cabin. That's when you and Daddy found me."

Katie smiled and looked over her shoulder at Reese. He lay perfectly still, his arms by his sides, but his eyes were open as he listened to their conversation. She caught his gaze and mouthed the words *thank you*. He gave a smile of contentment, then closed his eyes again.

Because she could see the movements of his breathing, Katie could tell he was just resting. But an urgency built within her. Reese said he was okay, but she wasn't so sure. She'd feel better once a medical doctor gave him a clean bill of health.

Three days later, Katie sat at the reception desk in the motel. Charlie had taken Chrissy with him to the grocery store. They'd spent so much time visiting Reese at the hospital in Carson City that they'd ignored their home life and had no milk or fresh produce.

Since it was the first of the month, Katie was printing checks to pay their bills. If she hurried, she could get them into the morning mail, but she was having trouble concentrating. All she could think about was that Reese would be getting out of the hospital today and she might never see him again. When she'd spoken to him yesterday afternoon, he was doing well. It would take time for his wounds to heal, but he'd be able to work soon. Because he'd been in so much pain since the fire, she hadn't yet talked with him about what was really on her mind.

She loved him. In fact, she'd never stopped loving him all these long, lonely years. But she couldn't tell him that. Not unless he felt the same about her.

"Hi, there."

Katie spun around, surprised to find him standing in the doorway. She blinked, thinking it must be a mirage. But no, he walked over to the counter, dressed in a loose shirt that didn't constrict the bandages she knew he had covering the burns on his back and shoulders. His faded blue jeans hugged his long legs like a second skin, and a jagged thatch of hair fell over his high forehead. The cowboy boots on his feet accented his rugged good looks. He fit perfectly in this community. A down-to-earth firefighter who was so strong and capable that her heart melted at the first sight of him.

And then she noticed he carried a large bouquet of roses. Red. At least two dozen.

"What…what are you doing here?" she asked.

He shrugged and gave her a lazy smile that made her heart beat faster. "I came to see you."

"But I thought you were getting out of the hospital today and going to Reno."

"My plans have changed. Sean picked me up at the hospital this morning and gave me a ride home."

Home. Hearing him say that word warmed her heart and brought a flush of heat to her face.

She tilted her head, thinking she must sound incoherent. But his presence here made her feel nervous and deliriously happy. "Home…as in here in Minoa, or here at the Cowboy Country Inn?"

He took a step closer. "My home is wherever you and Chrissy are. That's where I belong."

Her heart gave a powerful thump. "I don't understand, Reese. What's going on?"

Her senses went on high alert as he walked around the counter, moving slowly, telling her that he wasn't fully healed from the fire yet. She stood up to meet him, mesmerized by his green eyes.

"These are for you." He held out the roses.

On autopilot, she took them, the paper crackling as her fingers tightened around the long stems. "What are they for?"

"They're for the woman I love."

She took a quick inhalation, her legs feeling suddenly weak. Fearing she might drop the flowers, she smelled their sweet fragrance, then set them aside on the desk. "They're beautiful, Reese. But please don't tease me."

He shook his head, holding her gaze so intensely that she couldn't look away to save her life. He reached out and rested his hands on her bare arms. His palms felt solid and warm against her skin.

"We have a lot to talk about," he said.

"We do?"

"Yes. First, Sean told me that the investigation team discovered a cigar was the incendiary device that started the wildfire. And the license plate of the blue sedan definitely belongs to Bruce Miller. He's admitted to the police that he was up on Cove Mountain, trying to spy on me. Apparently he damaged his car and couldn't find the cabin, so he left. He threw his cigar butt out the car window. The investigators believe it smoldered in the tall grass along the roadside before igniting. He's facing fines and possible incarceration for the damage he's caused."

Ah, just as she'd suspected.

"So, I'm guessing he'll finally leave you alone, right?" she asked.

"Right."

"And what else did you want to talk about?"

"Us. I've accepted Sean's job offer. I'm going to be a captain on the Minoa Hotshot Crew."

She frowned, a sudden feeling of doubt filling her mind. "Are you sure that's wise?"

"I am. I thought I could never fight fires again. But then I was forced into a situation where I had to save my family's lives. I almost lost everything that means anything to me, but the Lord gave me a second chance. He helped me realize that I love fighting fires. That I'm good at it and that I want to keep doing it."

"Oh, Reese, I'm so happy to hear that." And she was. No matter what happened between them, she wanted him to be happy. To be content and at peace.

"I love you, Katie. When I think about how stupid I was and all the years we've lost, and what I put you and my mother through, I can't tell you enough how sorry I am. But it's true, Katie. I'm so very sorry for all the time we could have been together and I wasted the opportunity. Sorry for ever hurting you. I wish I could take it back. I'm a different man now. Believe me when I say I regret every wrong I've ever done. And please forgive me."

She didn't know what to say. She wanted to pinch herself, just to make sure she wasn't dreaming all this. "There's nothing to forgive, Reese. I'm sorry, too. I wish now that I had never written that article about your hotshot crew. If I hadn't written it, Tom Klarch never would have been able to publish it."

Reese pulled her against his chest. She didn't resist as he rested his chin on top of her head. Beneath her open palm, she felt the solid beating of his heart. He smelled subtly of spicy aftershave and licorice.

"That's true, but I'm glad you wrote about it now. You handled it with grace and finesse. It was a touching tribute to my hotshot team," he said.

"Do you really mean that?"

He kissed her forehead. "I do, Katie. I love you. So very much. And I want to live worthy of those men who died that day."

"Oh, Reese. And I love you. I always have. I always will."

"That's all I needed to hear." He released her and stepped back, taking her hand. Gripping the desk with his free hand, he lowered himself to one knee. Confused by his actions, Katie stared in awe.

"Kathleen Ashmore, you've taught me so much. You've taught me about faith and prayer and that I have a choice. I can choose who and what I want to be in this life. And I want to be a better man, for you and our daughter. You are my compass, my true north. With you and God by my side, I know I can find my way. I want you to go to school, to finally fulfill your dreams. Together, we can make that happen."

Katie licked her lips, hardly able to believe what she was hearing. School had been a distant dream she'd never believed could ever come true. But with Reese here in Minoa, all things seemed possible. She wasn't afraid anymore. Not of anything.

He reached inside his shirt pocket and pulled out a little black box. Opening it, he held it up for her inspection.

A modest diamond engagement ring rested on the velvet cover. It sparkled as morning sunlight streamed through the open window. Except for their daughter, Katie had never seen anything so lovely in her entire life.

"I want us to be a real family," he said. "Will you marry me, and make me the happiest man in the world?"

Tears of joy ran down Katie's face and she laughed out loud. "Oh, Reese! Yes, yes! A thousand times, yes!"

She helped him stand and then she was in his arms. He kissed her deeply and she cuddled close against his chest. And when he slid his ring onto her finger, she knew they'd both come home. Finally, together, they were right where they belonged. In each other's arms. Forever.

* * * * *

Dear Reader,

We were each sent here to earth to learn obedience to God's will, to keep His commandments and to learn to live by faith. But sometimes, that is easier said than done.

In this story, Reese Hartnett returns to his hometown, seeking answers and solace after losing his entire hotshot crew during a wildfire. After being raised by an abusive alcoholic father, Reese turned his back on God and has lived a lonely life free of good works and service to others.

When we face trials in our lives, it's easy to cling to our hurt, anger and pride. When we humble ourselves, that is when the Lord can do His greatest work in our lives. The power of prayer is great and the power of repentance is real and absolute.

I hope you enjoy reading this story and I invite you to visit my website at www.leighbale.com to learn more about my books.

May you find peace in the Lord's words!
Leigh Bale

COMING NEXT MONTH FROM
Love Inspired®

Available April 17, 2018

THE WEDDING QUILT BRIDE

Brides of Lost Creek • by Marta Perry

Widowed single mom Rebecca Mast returns to her Amish community hoping to open a quilt shop. She accepts carpenter Daniel King's offer of assistance—but she isn't prepared for the bond he forms with her son. Will getting closer expose her secret—or reveal the love she has in her heart for her long-ago friend?

THE AMISH WIDOW'S NEW LOVE

by Liz Tolsma

To raise money for her infant son's surgery, young Amish widow Naomi Miller must work with Elam Yoder—the man she once hoped to wed before he ran off. Elam's back seeking forgiveness—and a second chance with the woman he could never forget.

THE RANCHER'S SECRET CHILD

Bluebonnet Springs • by Brenda Minton

Marcus Palermo's simple life gets complicated when he meets the son he never knew he had—and his beautiful guardian. Lissa Hart thought she'd only stick around long enough to aid Marcus in becoming a dad—but could her happily-ever-after lie with the little boy and the rugged rancher?

HER TEXAS COWBOY

by Jill Lynn

Still nursing a broken heart since Rachel Maddox left town—and him—years earlier, rancher next door Hunter McDermott figures he can at least be cordial during her brief return. But while they work together on the Independence Day float, he realizes it's impossible to follow through on his plan because he's never stopped picturing her as his wife.

HOMETOWN REUNION

by Lisa Carter

Returning home, widowed former Green Beret Jaxon Pruitt is trying to put down roots and reconnect with his son. Though he took over the kayak shop his childhood friend Darcy Parks had been saving for, she shows him how to bond with little Brody—and finds herself wishing to stay with them forever.

AN UNEXPECTED FAMILY

Maple Springs • by Jenna Mindel

Cam Zelinsky never imagined himself as a family man—especially after making some bad choices in his life. But in seeking redemption, he volunteers to help single mom Rose Dean save her diner—and soon sees she and her son are exactly who he needs for a happy future.

LOOK FOR THESE AND OTHER LOVE INSPIRED BOOKS WHEREVER BOOKS ARE SOLD, INCLUDING MOST BOOKSTORES, SUPERMARKETS, DISCOUNT STORES AND DRUGSTORES.

LICNM0418

SPECIAL EXCERPT FROM

Love Inspired®

Widowed single mom Rebecca Mast returns to her Amish community hoping to open a quilt shop. She accepts carpenter Daniel King's offer of assistance—but she isn't prepared for the bond he forms with her son. Will getting closer expose her secret—or reveal the love she has in her heart for her long-ago friend?

Read on for a sneak preview of THE WEDDING QUILT BRIDE by Marta Perry, *available May 2018 from Love Inspired!*

"Do you want to make decisions about the rest of the house today, or just focus on the shop for now?"

"Just the shop today," Rebecca said quickly. "It's more important than getting moved in right away."

"If I know your *mamm* and *daad*, they'd be happy to have you stay with them in the *grossdaadi* house for always, ain't so?"

"That's what they say, but we shouldn't impose on them."

"Impose? Since when is it imposing to have you home again? Your folks have been so happy since they knew you were coming. You're not imposing," Daniel said.

Rebecca stiffened, seeming to put some distance between them. "It's better that I stand on my own feet. I'm not a girl any longer." She looked as if she might want to add that it wasn't his business.

No, it wasn't. And she certain sure wasn't the girl he remembered. Grief alone didn't seem enough to account for the changes in her. Had there been some other problem, something he didn't know about in her time away or in her marriage?

He'd best mind his tongue and keep his thoughts on business, he told himself. He was the last person to know anything about marriage, and that was the way he wanted it. Or if not wanted, he corrected honestly, at least the way it had to be.

"I guess we should get busy measuring for all these things, so I'll know what I'm buying when I go to the mill." Pulling out his steel measure, he focused on the boy. "Mind helping me by holding one end of this, Lige?"

The boy hesitated for a moment, studying him as if looking at the question from all angles. Then he nodded, taking a few steps toward Daniel, who couldn't help feeling a little spurt of triumph.

Daniel held out an end of the tape. "If you'll hold this end right here on the corner, I'll measure the whole wall. Then we can see how many racks we'll be able to put up."

Daniel measured, checking a second time before writing the figures down in his notebook. His gaze slid toward Lige again. It wondered him how the boy came to be so quiet and solemn. He certain sure wasn't like his *mammi* had been when she was young. Could be he was still having trouble adjusting to his *daadi*'s dying, he supposed.

Rebecca was home, but he sensed she had brought some troubles with her. As for him…well, he didn't have answers. He just had a lot of questions.

LIEXP0418

SPECIAL EXCERPT FROM

Love Inspired® SUSPENSE

With her serial killer brother out of prison and on the lam, can Staff Sergeant Zoe Sullivan prove she's not his accomplice before it's too late?

Read on for a sneak preview of
BOUND BY DUTY by Valerie Hansen,
the next book in the ***MILITARY K-9 UNIT*** *miniseries, available May 2018 from Love Inspired Suspense!*

She was being watched. Constantly. Every fiber of her being knew it. Lately she felt as though she was the defenseless prey and packs of predators were circling her and her helpless little boy, which was why she'd left Freddy home with a sitter. Were things as bad as they seemed? It was more than possible, and Staff Sergeant Zoe Sullivan shivered despite the warm spring day.

Scanning the busy parking lot as she left the Canyon Air Force Base Exchange with her purchases, Zoe quickly spotted one of the Security Forces investigators. Her pulse jumped, and hostility took over her usually amiable spirit. The K-9 cop in a blue beret and camo ABU—Airman Battle Uniform—was obviously waiting for her. She bit her lip. Nobody cared how innocent she was. Being the half sister of Boyd Sullivan, the escaped Red Rose Killer, automatically made her a person of interest.

LISEXP0418

Zoe clenched her teeth. There was no way she could prove herself so why bother trying? She squared her slim shoulders under her off-duty blue T-shirt and stepped out, heading straight for the Security Forces man and his imposing K-9, a black-and-rust-colored rottweiler.

Clearly he saw her coming because he tensed, feet apart, body braced. In Zoe's case, five and a half feet was the most height she could muster. The dark-haired tech sergeant she was approaching looked to be almost a foot taller.

He gave a slight nod as she drew near and greeted her formally. "Sergeant Sullivan."

Linc Colson's firm jaw, broad shoulders and strength of presence were familiar. They had met during a questioning session conducted by Captain Justin Blackwood and Master Sergeant Westley James shortly after her half brother had escaped from prison.

Zoe stopped and gave the cop an overt once-over, checking his name tag. "Can I help you with something, Sergeant Colson?"

Don't miss
BOUND BY DUTY by Valerie Hansen,
available May 2018 wherever
Love Inspired® Suspense books and ebooks are sold.

www.LoveInspired.com

LISEXP0418